# Scarred Loyalties

### Sins of the Underworld, Volume 2

Lena Blake

Published by Lena Blake, 2024.

Copyright © 2024 by Lena Blake

All rights reserved.

No part of this book may be reproduced, distributed, or transmitted in any form or by any means, including photocopying, recording, or other electronic or mechanical methods, without the prior written permission of the author, except in the case of brief quotations in book reviews.

This is a work of fiction. Names, characters, places, and incidents are the product of the author's imagination or are used fictitiously. Any resemblance to actual events, organizations, locales, or persons, living or dead is coincidental and is not intended by the authors.

Copyright © 2024 by Lena Blake

All rights reserved.

No part of this book may be reproduced, distributed, or transmitted in any form or by any means, including photocopying, recording, or other electronic or mechanical methods, without the prior written permission of the author, except in the case of brief quotations in book reviews.

This is a work of fiction. Names, characters, places, and incidents are the product of the author's imagination or are used fictitiously. Any resemblance to actual events, organizations, locales, or persons, living or dead is coincidental and is not intended by the authors.

# PROLOGUE

## Sienna

I wasn't afraid of the dark. My eyes were accustomed to the absence of light, and most of the time, it was a blessing for them. The monsters that used to scare children when they went to bed were not the ones that haunted me. They didn't live under the bed.

The monster in my life lived *on* my bed. On my mattress. Between my sheets.

He came at night, religiously, whenever he was home. He would cover my mouth and tell me to be a good girl, stay quiet, and please him because he was the conductor of my destiny. He was the master of my future.

I wanted to silence his voice in my ear, forget the weight of his hands on me, but it was the ghosts that pursued me. And it had nothing to do with turning on the lights. They still appeared when the entire room was illuminated.

So that at that moment, when I came home—if I could even call that miserable apartment in Central City, one of the worst neighborhoods in New Orleans, where I had come to live—a home, after a long night of work, he still screamed inside me. The clock read four in the morning, and I was eager to take off the wig that was itching my scalp and to remove the huge heels from my feet.

I turned the key twice in the lock and bolted it, because it was never too much, and finally took that thing off my head.

It wasn't very effective protection, I knew that, but my natural hair attracted too much attention. I could dye it, I could cut it, but it was the last good memory I had of my mother. It was what made me look like the only person I loved in the world.

The only person I knew who didn't betray me.

I went to my room, already barefoot, already accustomed to how small and claustrophobic the apartment was. For a girl who had always lived in a mansion and who had chances to marry rich men—having been engaged to the boss of the Cosa Nostra in Chicago, with rumors that I could marry the boss of New York and... well... who dreamed of the opportunity to join the heir of Los Angeles—that place must have felt like a prison.

For me, it was the first glimpse of freedom I had. Nothing had imprisoned me more than the mafia. Being free from it was almost like being able to fly, even though I still needed to keep my feet on the ground, with my wings hidden, until I saved enough money to go further away.

And I knew what I needed to do to make money faster. The offer had been made since I joined that club, where I danced, stripping for money.

I threw myself on the bed with that in mind. I was tired of feeling scared because I still felt too close. I needed to leave the United States and seek asylum in another country, preferably Ireland, where my mother still had some family.

While I lay there, staring at the ceiling, I opened my bag and took out my phone. It was a simple, second-hand model that I bought after selling some of the jewelry I managed to bring with me, in search of news.

Everything was very discreet in the world we lived in. People couldn't go around spreading the lives of the mobsters. Any journalist who dared to expose the truth would disappear. Anyone who reported the *famiglias* would also.

Still, I managed to stay informed. And there it was: Bruno Esposito had been found dead, and his sister, Sienna, is missing.

Of course, the news didn't give the exact details of the situation. They didn't say that my brother was tortured and killed because he tried to kill Kiara, the wife of one of the most powerful men in Chicago. It didn't mention that I had to flee at the first opportunity that arose, during my engagement to Giovanni, taking only the clothes on my back and the jewelry that, luckily, was with me. I wouldn't have been able to eat if not for that.

I had already imagined he would be dead, but the confirmation shouldn't have given me so much hope. He was my brother... for God's sake! I had been taught to love my family above all things, but all I wanted was for him to be dead.

The things he made me do. The way he tarnished my name. How he destroyed my entire life.

The way he almost killed Kiara, who was the only friend I had... although I could swear she never saw me that way, because I could never get close enough...

I threw the phone aside and put both hands to my face. My shoulders began to shake, and soon I was almost convulsing with sobs.

Not a cry of mourning. A cry of relief.

I was still not free. If the Cosa Nostra found me, I would be tortured and wouldn't be able to prove my innocence. Not alone, without resources, and without someone to protect me.

But I'd rather die than fall back into the hands of my greatest nightmare. He couldn't hurt me anymore. Never again.

# CHAPTER ONE

## Enrico

"*I swear upon this dagger of omertà, with the tip wet with blood, and before the honorable society, to be faithful to my companions and to renounce father, mother, sisters, and brothers, and to fulfill all my duties, even with blood if necessary.*"

The Cosa Nostra was like a demanding lover.

No matter how much you gave it all your life; no matter how much you donated your blood and loyalty to the rules and everything it stood for, it was never enough.

Since I discovered what kind of organization my family was part of; or rather, since I began to understand what it meant to be the heir to such a dark, mysterious, and criminal society, I followed its rhythm, its precepts, and obeyed it like a religion. I honored it, protected it, and respected it. More than a lover, it was like a wife.

One day I found myself eager to be part of it, to be accepted. To be worthy of working among people I so admired, including my father.

I was fourteen when I realized it wasn't a matter of admiration, but an imposition. It was around this time that I realized everything was much darker than what I saw in movies. Much less glamorous and interesting than I had imagined.

Still, even with scars on my body and soul, reminding me every day of who I was and what I should do, I never considered the possibility of not being loyal to it, because it was my legacy. I was the heir to unimaginable power.

Nothing would stop me from maintaining this conviction.

Or rather... almost nothing.

Just her.

*She* was capable of destabilizing the firm conviction I always had.

Always *she*...

I met Sienna Esposito shortly after my initiation. The scars that still lived within me at that time, even as an adult, were still too recent. At sixteen, two years after seeing hell up close, although the wounds had healed, I did not feel they were cured. I became withdrawn, gloomy, and disillusioned. All I wanted was to blend in with the darkness.

Or perhaps I was just like her, because I felt her within me, in every part of my body.

It was an eleven-year-old girl who made me smile for the first time. She was the only one who had the courage to stand by my side, with her long red hair and a beaming smile, when everyone seemed to avoid me as if I had a contagious disease. The boys my age didn't understand why I felt so suffocated.

Their parents hadn't initiated them or given them training like mine. I came back home intact, missing not a single piece, by a narrow margin.

Only the little girl with the red hair, my *scarlatta*, as I called her, could penetrate the wall I built around myself, winning my heart.

Little by little, we started meeting at every event we attended, and she always comforted me with her sweet demeanor and innocence, which I feared would be corrupted.

How foolish I was... of course, she couldn't stay intact forever.

On the first day I saw the same darkness in her eyes that I recognized in mine, I wanted to kill whoever had destroyed her. For a while, I believed it was mourning for the death of her parents, but gradually I realized it was the fear she felt from her brother.

I fought to get our marriage negotiated so that she wouldn't end up in anyone else's hands but mine. I didn't know if she loved me, if she had feelings for me as I had for her, but I could swear I would never treat her like any of the others—as if she were an object.

Bruno Esposito, however, never considered me as a husband for his sister. I suspected he didn't want her to be with someone he had any interest in, but I could never be sure. Especially since after I made the proposal, we never managed to get close again. She seemed like a scared little animal from then on, not even looking at me.

Even in the face of this defeat, seeing her flourish and attract everyone's attention but never being able to be mine, I remained loyal to the *famiglia*, acting as expected of me.

I always knew that if I ever needed to betray the Cosa Nostra, it would be for her. For the woman I loved.

When the story began that she was a traitor like the damned brother, I never needed confirmation to be completely sure of the truth.

Sienna was innocent. But to prove it, I needed to find her. And I needed to do it as discreetly as possible because if anyone suspected my investigation, she would be in danger.

I couldn't trust anyone; it had to be me doing the work. Not to mention, there wasn't a single person who knew her like I did.

I knew where she had gone. New Orleans... as the Anne Rice fan she was. From the way she always discussed the stories with me, I never doubted what her destination would be. Adding to that the fact that I recognized the jewel she was wearing the day she disappeared, I was able to piece things together.

However, I didn't like what I discovered.

It was by following her that I found out she was working in a club with a dubious reputation. Not one like the one Dominic Ungaretti managed, which, although it was a den of lust and perversion, was frequented by people from the highest ranks of the Cosa Nostra hierarchy. The girls who worked and danced there had some form of respect, of protection.

Sienna was showcasing her body on a stage every night, gyrating on a pole, wearing a wig, at the mercy of the worst filth possible.

She was vulnerable, unprotected, probably believing that a blonde wig would keep her incognito.

And perhaps it would. Maybe I was the one who looked at her the most, all the time, and could recognize her even in a crowd. But her beauty was not trivial. It was not forgettable. I could swear that many of the men who had surrounded her in the past, from soldiers to capos and bosses from all states, none of them could ignore her face.

Sienna's beauty had always been a curse for her.

I stayed at the back of the club on the first day, just observing, fearing she might see me and be frightened by my presence. I wanted to believe she would trust me, that she wouldn't suspect I meant her harm or would turn her in, but I couldn't be sure.

She went by the name Scarlett. From the start, I tried to think she remembered me fondly, but I doubted it, considering she must have hated every minute of that job, yet she still used the nickname I gave her.

I sat with a glass of whiskey in hand, ready to watch her dance. I swore I would look at her with respect, because my feelings for Sienna were deep enough for me to revere her to that extent. My intentions had always been to marry her and only then to make her mine. She was sacred, untouchable before we went to the altar.

For a long time, I condemned my thoughts, and at that moment I felt the same way. Yet I couldn't even begin to control myself when she turned her back, her sensual movements making her waist look like waves in a stormy sea.

Like her face, Sienna's body was not just beautiful. She seemed sculpted in every detail. Made for sin. She was not a small or scantily endowed woman. She was tall, had hips, breasts, a slim waist, a flat stomach, and toned legs.

She was much more beautiful than my imagination could ever sketch.

And I had sketched her a million times, with hands that liked to make art in the most clandestine way the world I lived in allowed.

I took a deep breath, taking a generous sip of my drink, hoping the alcohol would numb my senses enough for me to forget where I was and what I was needing to see.

When I returned to my hotel, I was more than convinced that I needed to reveal myself to Sienna, to tell her my intentions and offer my protection; giving her the chance to leave that place.

Still, I kept returning to that place night after night, like an addict seeking his fix. Lacking the courage to approach, I feared she would run away and not give me the chance to explain.

I could have continued like this for more days, were it not for the fact that the host of that dive appeared on stage after Sienna's performance, bringing her by the arm as if she were merchandise, with a microphone, announcing:

"Ladies and gentlemen, look... I have a surprise for you. Our untouchable Scarlett will be auctioned off today. Open your wallets, because it's a one-in-a-million chance. This precious gem here will finally let someone enjoy the beautiful thing between her legs all night long."

And with those vulgar and disgusting words, everyone started shouting, banging on the tables, and applauding the decision that left me completely mortified.

# CHAPTER TWO

## Sienna

"No!" I swore the word would come out as a scream, strong and resonant, but it was nothing more than a terrified whisper.

John Mister – as he called himself, just as I began to call myself Scarlett without needing to show a single document – was the pimp who managed the girls at the club. Not just those who sold their bodies, but also those who danced. From the first moment I stepped into that dive, and by the way he looked at me, I always knew he would torment me to push me further.

I never thought, however, that the day would come when he would force me.

"No! You can't do this!" I managed to raise my voice a little, allowing it to be heard.

The moment he turned his face toward me, still holding the microphone, with all those people shouting, laughing, and reaching out to touch me, crowding around the stage, I could smell the strong scent of alcohol coming from his mouth.

It wasn't common for him to get drunk during what he called working hours because he swore to look after the girls' safety. Still, there he was, with red eyes and a terrible stench.

"You're going to have to go along with it, sweetheart. I got an eviction notice earlier today. I don't have anything more valuable here than that little pussy of yours..."

He couldn't be serious. All the girls who worked as prostitutes agreed to his terms. Not only that... they needed the money and went there specifically for what they did.

With me, it was different because I had always made it clear that it wasn't my intention. I didn't even like dancing, but it was the only job that opened doors for me without asking questions and allowed me to pay my rent and food. They had never stopped trying to convince me, but that was all.

"John, please... you can't force me."

"I gave you a job and a chance. You owe me that! And you'll make money too. I guarantee you're not a virgin, so it won't even hurt."

I wasn't a virgin, indeed. But all I knew about sex was painful, shameful, cruel, and very sordid. It was never consensual, never pleasurable. I couldn't allow myself to be touched again without my consent.

To be honest, the last thing I wanted to accept after becoming truly free was for a man to touch me. I just wanted to live a quiet, peaceful, solitary, discreet life, in a clean and comfortable little house, and have the company of a cat. That was my dream.

One of the girls, probably outraged by the situation, came to me with a robe. I had no idea to whom it belonged, but it smelled of cheap perfume. At that moment, I clung to the fabric as if it were a lifeboat. Being nearly naked at that moment made everything even more terrifying.

"Ready?" John shouted again, and I tried to pull away from his hand, but I was held tighter.

I realized very easily that it was pointless to struggle. I wouldn't be freed from this ordeal, especially since he seemed desperate. He wasn't an honorable man, and I should have known that from the first moment I stepped into that place and agreed to work for him. Even my payment was a disgrace, but I had to accept it in silence because I was a fugitive.

In fact, most of the girls there were also fugitives. Some had escaped abusive husbands, others were ex-convicts, and others just needed to survive in a world completely unjust to women.

Thinking about that, I took a deep breath and let the coldest version of myself take over. The one trained by Bruno Esposito, former consigliere of the New York mafia, in the worst possible way, to not show my emotions.

"You're going to pay for this, John. It wasn't what we agreed on," I whispered, as controlled as possible. Not showing my emotions was the rule. If it didn't affect me, I wouldn't give them the satisfaction of celebrating my downfall.

"Do you have a contract? No, you don't. So now this is the deal. Just once, sweetheart. You'll see it'll be worth it. It'll be fifty percent for each of us."

"No! I don't..."

I barely managed to finish speaking before he started goading the "audience":

"Let's start with a bid of a thousand dollars?"

I swore that no one there could pay that much money for a night with me, but a man in his sixties raised his hand, licking his lips and looking at me as if I were a succulent and delicious delicacy.

I even shuddered, not only from that look but especially because the bids kept increasing exponentially.

We reached ten thousand dollars, fifteen, twenty.

What was happening?

They were having fun, on top of everything, and I looked from side to side, trying to keep control.

I had lost my fear of sex a long time ago. After being hurt in every possible way and abused for years and years, what my brother called our midnight meetings, and then others orchestrated by him, became trivial. I would just close my eyes and try to transport myself to other places, focus my thoughts on anything else. I didn't always succeed. Most of the time, yes.

I wouldn't be able to escape that place. Not at that moment, at least. If there was any chance, it would be after the auction, but I imagined I would have to endure.

It would be just one night. Afterward, I would leave. Disappear. Take the money and my things and move to another city, another place. I could start over in another club or doing something else. I wouldn't make as much as a waitress, but it could be good. I could have a fairer work schedule and get the kitten I so wanted.

I remained silent, imagining that new life, when something caught my attention.

A new bid. The final one. One I knew no one would cover.

"One hundred thousand dollars."

The entire room fell silent. Everyone turned toward the table from which the voice had come.

I knew that voice... But it couldn't be.

I finally opened my eyes, coming out of my trance, and stared at the man all in black who was sitting at the back.

A man with straight hair, brushed to the side, reaching down to the base of his neck. The man with the most intense blue eyes I knew. The eyes that had looked at me with the most tenderness since my mother died.

At that moment, his brow was furrowed as if he were angry.

Angry at me? Could it be?

There was Enrico Preterotti, the only man capable of affecting me.

But he was obviously there to take the traitor of the Cosa Nostra. He was probably sent because they knew I trusted him.

I couldn't allow that.

# CHAPTER THREE

## Sienna

Everyone remained silent for very little time, until John himself, who seemed a bit dazed, moved and used the microphone again:

"But... but... Wow! Wow!"—dazed, he stammered and seemed not to know what to say. "Did I hear that right? One hundred thousand dollars?"

A light illuminated Enrico from where he was, and I noticed that he was staring at me intently, even while responding with a nod to someone else.

"I don't even know what to do or say, folks. Is anyone going to cover our friend in black's offer?"

While everyone whispered and John waited for a response, Enrico and I continued our silent exchange of glances. Neither of us looked away, probably each for our own reasons.

It was good to see him. It would be even better if I weren't so certain he was there to drag me from one hell to an even worse one.

"So we have our lucky guy. Or rather... a good man makes his own luck, don't you agree?"—John laughed easily, probably because the amount he was set to gain, if he truly followed through on his promise to split the money with me, could really make a difference in his problem.

Completely stunned, I couldn't hear anything else around me, not even when John ordered two of the club's security guards to come closer and literally drag me up to the second floor, to one of the rooms where the girls attended to "clients."

They had a very tacky décor, with red satin sheets, black and gold details, and I had never been inside one of them.

Much less had I ever been locked inside one.

I stood still, staring at the door, without any reaction. Rationally speaking, screaming like a madwoman wouldn't help, because no one would come to my aid. Most of the girls, if they could, would undoubtedly do that. Contrary to what many might think, there was no jealousy among them. They helped each other as much as they could, especially in difficult times.

I felt a bit more detached because my job was different, but none ever excluded me. I would probably miss them if I managed to get out, and if I could help them someday, I would do so without a second thought.

But to get out of there, I had to act on my own.

If I feared being forced to have sex with a stranger, facing Enrico would be even more frightening. Because I knew he wasn't paying all that money to take me to bed. He would drag me out of that place and take me straight to a warehouse, at the mercy of Giovanni Caccini and Dominic Ungaretti.

The rooms weren't prisons. I might be locked inside one, but I knew there were no bars on the windows. I also knew roughly the building's layout, with its ledges and the height of each floor.

I was athletic and had a flexible body. The option to fall and injure myself was still better than being tortured by a Cosa Nostra boss. Than being condemned and remembered for something I never did.

I went for the window, making as little noise as possible, carefully opening the glass, and looking down. Indeed, the height wasn't the worst, but in my nervousness, I forgot something very relevant that would be of great help: there was a balcony with bars that I could use for support until I reached the first floor.

I didn't think twice, much less about the fact that I was only wearing a robe over my almost naked body. Much less about how cold it was outside.

Again... a cold or even hypothermia was still a better option than what awaited me in the hands of the mafia.

I descended like a cat burglar, ready for a heist, very carefully, cursing myself for not taking off my high heels. That was a factor that complicated the descent, but I continued without hesitation, climbing down the bars and reaching the first floor.

As soon as my feet hit the ground, I ran. This time, I didn't stop to worry about my shoes, at least not initially, because I couldn't afford to waste time. I was trained to walk gracefully in any circumstance, and running wouldn't be a problem.

I sped through the streets of New Orleans, which had become my home, even though it wasn't what I would choose for my coming years, safe and comfortable.

I knew those streets well. I knew I would need to cross an avenue to get to my home. Depending on what happened, I might try to escape from there and not even go to get my things, especially since my purse and cell phone were left at the club. But there was money under my mattress—the most cliché thing I could do—and I couldn't leave it behind.

Someone was following me; I knew that. I could see a shadow, hear some movements. It wasn't someone given to making noise, so I assumed it wasn't one of the club's henchmen.

It was Enrico, I was sure. I could even swear I recognized his footsteps, even though our interactions had never been as frequent and close as I would have liked.

And if it was him, I was in serious trouble because that man would catch me. One way or another. The predator-prey game had gotten too serious and dangerous.

I noticed he was getting closer, so I sped up even more. Still in my shoes, trying to balance as best I could and feeling my calves burning.

I couldn't wait for the light to change. If I did, if I stopped, Enrico would get closer and closer. If he reached out, he would be able to grab me.

A car was coming. But it was all or nothing.

In another very dark comparison, being hit by a car was still better than what awaited me.

Even so, I couldn't escape. I was about to step onto the avenue when my arm was grabbed.

Enrico pulled me toward him, and I lost my balance a little because of the shoe, which made him wrap an arm around my waist.

I had no more chances. He wouldn't let me escape under any circumstances.

His lips parted, and I felt his warm breath on my face. For a few moments, I swore he was going to say something, but he gave up midway. He seemed hypnotized, reverent... relieved.

He raised his hand, encircling me and pulling off my wig, as well as the pins holding my heavy hair. He took them out one by one, patiently, as if we weren't in the middle of the street, letting the world pass by around us.

"Don't run away from me"—that's what he said.

What else could I do?

I needed to deceive him, show submission, stay calm, and find the right moment to trick him.

But how could I escape from the darkness itself?

# CHAPTER FOUR

## Enrico

My Sienna...
 As her hair was revealed, after I tore off that ridiculous blonde and almost white wig, throwing it to the ground, I let out a heavy sigh. Both of relief and despair.

I wasn't used to giving in so easily to my feelings, but she had a way of bringing them to the surface that made them impossible to ignore.

Knowing she was alive was like salvation, because I didn't feel capable of continuing to exist in a world that she wasn't a part of. At the same time, having her with me made me absolutely certain that from that moment on, I would do everything I could to keep her safe and away from those who might want to harm her.

"Scarlatta..." I whispered, taking the same hand that had removed her wig to her face, caressing it.

I had no right to touch her. I never did, actually. Not even when we were two boys did I dare to touch her, because I always feared contaminating her with my darkness; with how dark I felt. Later, even knowing she had her own share of melancholy and suffering, though I didn't know why, I still didn't feel worthy.

At that moment, however, it was just us. We were like two outsiders in a world that only took and never gave us anything.

Destiny owed us a lot.

"Did you come to get me for them?" she asked, while I still touched her, feeling half foolish, half lost.

"I came to get you to protect you."

"What is protection to you?"

"Proving your innocence."

"How can you be so sure I'm not a traitor?"

I didn't answer. There were no coherent words that could explain *how* I knew. My heart had been forged to be cold and cruel, but the only answer to Sienna's question was that I believed in her.

The problem was, even if I didn't believe, I would still have the impulse to protect her.

"We're leaving here," I said firmly. I had made sure I hadn't been followed, and I would never allow anyone to reach her because of me, but it wasn't a good idea for us to stay there in the middle of the street.

If Sienna attracted attention on her own, the two of us together certainly wouldn't go unnoticed. In our circle, people knew us. Anyone could report us, and then both of us would be judged as traitors, without me even having the chance to help her.

"I'm not going with you, Enrico," she replied calmly, with that impassive face that dismantled me.

Sienna was a model of perfection. Both in her appearance and her behavior. I knew that she was considered by many to be the ideal wife for never speaking too loudly, for being elegant, dressing appropriately, laughing softly, and being the queen of good manners. But I knew her. I knew her sweeter, more playful, more silly side. She wasn't just the ice queen, as some had called her before all of this. She was much more.

At that moment, however, all I saw was the cold woman, shaped to be what everyone wanted her to be. She had never looked at me that way, but apparently, I had become just another person for her. The image of someone else she needed to fear.

"I don't think it's an option. I won't allow you to go back to the Cosa Nostra. Not to be killed. No matter what I have to do to keep you with me," I said again.

"Oh, of course. You bought me, didn't you?" Sienna might have used disdain to say this, but her voice sounded melodious and soft as always. Still, probably using the mask she wore amidst the Cosa Nostra.

I took a deep breath, feeling my patience wear thin. It wasn't the time to argue, much less to be lenient, even though Sienna deserved her behavior to be excused given the circumstances.

But if she wanted to treat me that way, she would be treated the same.

"Yes. I bought you."

She raised an eyebrow, but almost imperceptibly.

"You spent too much. In the environment you were in, you could have gotten what you wanted for much less"—the woman struggled to remain impassive, but I could feel that her perfectly lined jaw was slightly clenched.

The hand on her back tightened with a bit more force, because I was angry too.

The two heated individuals wouldn't be a good thing.

"You're worth every penny." Of course, I didn't want her to think it was a physical matter. Because, indeed, it wasn't. My phrase was about everything else.

To me, Sienna was worth all my fortune, as well as her safety and protection.

I didn't have time to hear her say anything, because I saw two men running in our direction. I recognized them as the ones who had forcibly taken Sienna off the stage. Although my urge was to pull out the gun from its holster and shoot both of them for how they had treated her, I couldn't draw attention to us.

I stepped back a bit and kept my hand on her arm, especially when I saw that the next vehicle coming down the avenue was a taxi.

"Let's go," I said in an authoritative tone and pulled her with me, stopping the car and getting in with her, leaving the damn blonde wig on the ground.

My car was parked a few blocks away, so I only asked the taxi to take a longer route, especially to further throw off anyone who might be watching us, either from the club or someone who had followed me and consequently reached her.

It was a quick ride, so I soon jumped out, taking her with me and pulling her towards my car.

"Enrico! What are you going to do? Where are you taking me?"

"Don't worry, I have everything under control, everything ready. Just trust me."

She clearly didn't trust me, but she didn't have much of a choice. The place we were in was dangerous, her feet must have been hurting from the heels, and she was only wearing a robe and lingerie in the cold, vulnerable to the eyes of everyone, to any kind of person.

"Get in the car, Sienna. *Per favore*.

I had the door open, waiting for her to decide. We didn't have much time for conversations, although we were a bit away from the club and in the dark, slightly protected from curious gazes.

"I escaped, Enrico. I survived when all the odds were against me. I managed to live and I want a decent life."

"I can help you prove your innocence."

"What ties me to the Cosa Nostra? I don't want anything from them."

"I can give you the life you want."

"Can you?" She didn't seem to believe anything I was saying, but I needed her to give me a chance. Sienna sighed, tired. "They will never leave me alone, will they?"

"I have plans, but I need you to listen to me. For that, you have to come with me."

"And if it's a trap?"

"If it were, I would have put you in this car a long time ago. I'm trying to do things your way because no one ever has."

That seemed to hit directly on her wound. It wasn't meant to be a statement made with the intention of blackmail, but it served to make her change her mind and accept my help.

With her in the car, I simply walked around, settling behind the wheel and driving off, hoping for a chance to talk, for her to listen to me, and for us to reach an agreement.

An agreement that might be dangerous for both of us, but it couldn't be any other way.

I had finally found her. So I couldn't let her get lost again.

# CHAPTER FIVE

## Sienna

I knew that Sienna all too well, the one who took over me as soon as I found myself at the mercy of Enrico Preterotti. Inside his car, with no choice but to accept whatever might come, not even knowing where he was taking me.

Just as I told him, I had fought to survive. Not just when I escaped from the Cosa Nostra, but when I hopped on countless buses, stopping from city to city, wearing a wig, trying to disguise myself in the best way possible, fearing for my life every second.

I fought too when I allowed myself to be completely degraded by going to that club every night and dancing for men who filled me with vulgar words and lewd looks; who often reached out and touched me without my permission.

But it was all worth it when I imagined being safe, away from everything that had hurt me up to that point. When I had the audacity to delude myself with the hope of a better life.

One of the problems of having Enrico back was starting to desire things that hadn't been my priority when I escaped. The first of these was clearing my name. Disassociating it from the image Bruno had left of our family. Honoring the Esposito surname, since I was the only one left.

The bigger problem of having Enrico back was remembering my childhood dreams of one day being happy with him.

I was no longer that girl. I no longer trusted people. Men. I didn't trust anyone who had power over me, who had enough strength to subjugate and control me again.

The only way I knew how to deal with this was by closing myself off. My brother Bruno taught me to be this way. He was my teacher in the worst way possible. Showing me in practice that the more indifferent I appeared to everything they did to me, the less pleasure they derived from it.

When he came to my bed and took me against my will, the more I struggled and showed suffering, the more pleasure he took. My indifference was my greatest weapon. Becoming invisible, uninteresting, and almost frigid helped me more than I could have hoped.

So I needed to embody the Ice Queen once again with the Shadow Knight – what a duo we made! – so that, perhaps, he would give up on me.

I stayed silent throughout the ride, even though I didn't know what our destination would be. Enrico wasn't much of a conversationalist either, which made the atmosphere very heavy in that claustrophobic space. At several moments, I wanted to open the door and jump out while the car was still moving, because I still didn't know what his choice would be. Even though his feelings for me had always been very evident, could his loyalty to the Cosa Nostra be so fragile as to be broken by a woman?

And, again, sending Enrico to fetch me seemed like a very good choice, considering that, out of everyone, he would be the one I would trust the most.

His eyes occasionally wandered over me, as if he wanted to say something, but knew that neither of us would make any hasty moves. We were two players on a very dark board, and both had already lost too much to make risky bets.

We arrived, however, at a hotel. Luxurious, like many I had stayed in, as the daughter of a powerful mafia family, although that was part of the past. Enrico got out, and I could have had my chance to escape, but he had intentionally locked the car.

I gave a bitter smile, thinking that, in a way, no matter how good his intentions were, I would end up becoming his prisoner as well.

He opened the door for me, and I stepped out. Considering I was once again taking on the role of the old Sienna, I was a bit embarrassed to enter the hotel dressed like this, in just a vulgar robe over lacy lingerie, but I didn't back down. I held my head high and walked alongside Enrico, who placed his hand on my back almost as if he wanted to make sure I stayed by his side.

The presidential suite was our destination, and it was practically a penthouse, with several rooms and two bedrooms. Enrico was visibly already staying there, as there were bags and other belongings scattered about, but in a very organized manner.

I slightly opened the curtain, checking the window. We were on the eighteenth floor, which made me smile provocatively.

"High enough so I won't escape through the window again?" I tried to ask with minimal emotions displayed.

"High enough because I wanted the best. This is the most comfortable and luxurious suite in the hotel. Not to mention it has two areas. I thought this way, I could give you a bit more privacy."

"You had a lot of confidence that you would reach me."

"I never doubted for a second," Enrico responded very confidently, as he removed his watch.

His gaze was fixed on me, and, as always, it was a testament to the intensity he emanated. I remained standing, in front of him, with my arms crossed, analyzing him.

"How did you find me?"

His broad shoulders sagged slightly inside that enormous, heavy overcoat, which gave me the impression that he was even more enormous than he actually was. A heavy sigh made his chest rise and fall, almost tiredly.

"I think I know more about you than I should. I never doubted fate. I knew it was New Orleans, because of the books you read..."

"Anne Rice. I always read them in secret..." I let a tone of nostalgia overtake me, even though I didn't want to show him anything. "And you remembered..."

"I saw the necklace you were wearing the day you disappeared. I went from pawn shop to pawn shop, then to jewelry stores. I found it in one of them; by chance the owner knew where you were... *working*." Enrico didn't even try to hide his disdain when talking about the club.

Of course, he didn't approve, and it wasn't his place to do so. It was my choice.

However, from that moment on, I no longer knew if he would have any power over my decisions.

He stepped away from me for a few moments, moving towards the room's safe. I watched his movements, trying to imagine how quickly he would catch up with me if I tried to pass him to get to the door. I also pondered if that would be a huge mistake; if I would be safer with him or outside.

In doubt, I thought it better to stay put.

I was surprised, however, when Enrico returned, bringing a velvet box in hand. When he opened it, I found my necklace; the same one I had sold for a pittance compared to what it was worth.

"I sold it," I said, realizing how trivial it sounded. He knew.

"And I bought it back. It's yours. You won. You shouldn't have to part with your things."

"But I had to."

"Not anymore."

I lifted my chin in a challenging manner.

"Why are you willing to support me?"

"For a while, yes."

"Oh... I had forgotten. You didn't just buy a necklace. You *bought* me entirely."

Keeping my eyes locked on the man in front of me, I moved my hands to the belt of my robe, slowly loosening it. Underneath, I was wearing only the lingerie I danced in, a dark green that I knew complemented me well, matching my hair color. It was loose, like a heavy curtain. There was still some makeup on my face, though I never used much, even for performances, but enough to give me a slightly different look, regardless of how many years passed.

A face that had always worked for the mafia, the image of innocence they liked, but wasn't as profitable for a den like the one where I worked.

I let the garment slide off my shoulders, falling down my arms and pooling on the floor. It was a garish mess of colors with Chinese prints, but I didn't even glance at it. My focus was still on Enrico.

I saw his pronounced Adam's apple move up and down, showing he had swallowed hard. Still, he was a decent opponent because he didn't take his eyes off my face.

"Make yourself comfortable. The product is yours," I whispered serenely, hiding the vulnerability I felt.

It wasn't a secret that I had feelings for Enrico. From the moment I met him, a delusion was born in the little girl I once was, a hope that our families would favor a union between us. I allowed myself to fall in love with him, even as Bruno started to show his dangerous side.

After my brother touched me for the first time, all I could think—besides the pain that comes with rape—was that I could no longer be worthy of becoming the wife of a man like Enrico, who seemed like a prince to me.

Yet, I kept falling deeper in love.

As I was violated time and again, the desire to love and be loved by a man scared me, and I began to leave it behind. When I fled, I had to force myself to accept that it was a distant dream. With that, I swore that what I felt for Enrico was left behind.

At that moment, I had no idea what would happen if he decided to go further. If he agreed with what I was proposing and took me to bed.

So when he came toward me, taking slow, almost predatory steps, with those narrow eyes fixed on mine, despite my body being almost completely exposed, I forced myself to ignore the shiver that ran down my spine, trying to imagine what it would feel like to experience something I hated—sex—with someone I actually felt something for.

Still, the fear was stronger. I had a horror of being touched intimately. Even when imagining those hands were Enrico's.

He knelt in front of me with an almost rehearsed elegance, and without taking his eyes off me, he gathered the garment, lifting it and redressing me with it.

With firm hands, he tied the belt around my waist, still keeping his eyes on mine. It was unsettling... the way he seemed more than determined not to look away. I didn't know his intention, but he was managing to destabilize me.

"There are limits a man can cross, Sienna. There are others he cannot. I won't dare look at you or touch you until I earn your trust."

"And what if that never happens?"

"Then you will always be untouchable to me."

His answer surprised me and even left me a little startled. I had always been taught that men cannot control their impulses, and that's why they can't be condemned for their actions. They're like animals, so they cheat, rape, take what they want without consent. Not that I personally justified any of that, but those were the excuses I heard many of them give.

Enrico always seemed different. While no one ever asked me what I wanted, he was there, paying attention and interested in my opinions. And at that moment, he was rejecting what I was offering him, with such conviction that it might have hurt my ego if I didn't know he truly desired me.

In those sublimely blue eyes was all the answer I might need.

I knew it wasn't just desire.

"Come, I'll show you to your room. It's better we sleep and rest. Tomorrow we need to travel."

"Where to?"

"Los Angeles..."

"You're insane... You can't take me back to the den of wolves. You'll kill me, Enrico." I continued to keep calm, hoping my argument would be stronger than his thoughts.

"I have a plan, but you'll have to trust me."

I didn't trust anyone, but I had no choice. At that moment, I was in Enrico Preterotti's hands, for better or for worse.

# CHAPTER SIX

## Enrico

I clearly wasn't going to be able to sleep. I didn't even have the desire to try. There was a huge bed waiting for me, with warm and fragrant sheets, but also dreams and a restlessness I wasn't ready to face.

Sitting in the leather armchair in the living room of the suite we'd taken, with a glass of whiskey in hand from a bottle I'd bought the night before, I sat still, staring into nothing, trying to give myself the chance to contemplate what had happened in the past few hours.

I had finally found Sienna. After so much waiting and anguish, she was just a few meters away. But more than that, she was safe.

I didn't know how long it would stay that way. The moment the Cosa Nostra found out, there would be no excuses, no chance to explain; she wouldn't only be taken from me, but would also be subjected to the cruelty I knew all too well.

Because it was a cruelty that *I* also practiced.

I closed my eyes for a few moments, finally absorbing the reality. I gripped the glass tightly, feeling the large ring I wore on my right pinky brush against the surface. I took another deep breath, as it was my way of trying to maintain control.

I took a sip, hoping the drink would warm my throat and numb me a bit so my thoughts would calm down. They never went silent, in fact, but at that moment they screamed that I was insane.

The plan was bold. More risky than anything I'd done before. Still... what wouldn't I do for her?

My ears were on high alert for movement in the bedroom because I knew that, no matter how well she could mask her emotions, Sienna was scared.

And how could she not be, considering everything she had been through?

I knew she had taken a shower, turned on the TV, watched for a while, but then remained completely silent. I didn't want to invade her privacy, but given the circumstances, anything could have happened. It would be impossible for her to escape, especially since I was near the only door to the room, and I didn't want her to feel like a prisoner with me, even though... Well... from that moment on, if she accepted my ideas, that would become her condition.

Not because of me. But because of the mafia. The world she was born into and raised in.

Concerned, I got up and went towards the bedroom. The door was slightly ajar, and I could have just looked through the crack, but from where I was, I couldn't see the bed.

I promised myself I'd only open it a little, just to check if she was actually sleeping, safe and sound, but the sight of her in that state caught my attention and nearly mesmerized me enough to step in and get closer.

I saw her sprawled on the bed, her red hair spread out. The robe was slightly open, revealing much more of her body than it should have. She seemed exhausted to the point of not even waking up when I removed her feet from the comforter so I could pull it over her and cover her.

Those were my excuses: making sure she was okay and covering her because the night was cold. There was nothing else to do there, but the need to look at her was much stronger. And I considered myself a man of strong will for most things.

As always, Sienna was the cause of all my unravellings. No matter how trivial they might seem, she always stirred something in me, always drew out the worst and the best in me.

I memorized every contour of her face; every delicate detail. I controlled the urge to touch her and caress her cheeks, rosy from the tranquility of sleep, adoring her with my eyes and still a bit dazed that she was there.

I went back to the living room, opened one of my suitcases, and took out a notebook and a small case containing only a simple pencil and an eraser. I sat on the sofa and leafed through the previous drawings. It had been a long time since there was anything new there; probably since Sienna disappeared.

Most of the images were of her. In various moments, various styles. Sometimes just her hand, sometimes a close-up of her neck, her back. She was my muse, my obsession.

I only stopped when dawn broke because I had to resolve an important matter. I knew the hotel's clothing store was open twenty-four hours a day and offered delivery service. I couldn't go down and take too long, much less leave Sienna locked in there without her own card to come and go. As long as I didn't believe *she* would trust and wait for my directions, hear my plan, and agree with it, I needed to keep an eye on her.

I ordered the simplest clothes possible. A pair of jeans and a T-shirt, even though they didn't match Sienna. I always saw her in elegant dresses, suits, and high heels, but I couldn't tell if that was how she liked to dress or if it was just another imposition she accepted without question.

They delivered in less than an hour, and I left the perfumed paper bag on the desk in the room where she had been sleeping, although she wasn't in bed anymore. I might have been worried if I hadn't heard movements inside the bathroom. Besides, she wouldn't have another way out but to pass by me.

I left the room and set up breakfast, which arrived with the girl from the clothing store. There were croissants, coffee, cake, and milk. I also ordered a piece of strawberry pie because I knew she liked it. It was always her favorite dessert since childhood.

It was, indeed, what she looked at first. I watched her expression, and her eyes lit up.

That was what I needed to pay attention to, but she appeared in a towel, with wet hair, without all the heavy makeup from the previous night.

The towel was large but covered at most halfway down her legs. Still, I had seen her in lingerie, on stage, which was far more revealing. The problem was that, in my perception, a towel seemed much more intimate; not to mention it was the first time I saw her with a clean face, and I could swear she was much more beautiful that way.

"Are you going to make me skip breakfast to eat the pie?" she joked, but with a melancholic humor. At least I had managed to get something out of her. Something that set her apart from the Sienna of others and brought her a little closer to mine.

"You can eat whatever you want, as long as you eat. And we can't delay, unfortunately. We have a flight to catch in three hours. There are clothes there, your size."

"How do you know my size?" she asked, but didn't even wait for me to answer, just looked at me seriously. How would I explain that I had spent years of my life watching her and memorizing every part of her? Realizing this, Sienna changed the subject: "Enrico, I can't go with you. I can't go to Los Angeles. Your family is loyal to Dominic and Giovanni... After everything that happened with Kiara, they..."

"They won't do anything against you because I won't let them. No one will know. The closer we are to the chaos, the less they will imagine. Besides, when we get to where you'll be staying, we'll talk about what I've been thinking."

"Why not now?"

"Because I need a place that I know is safe, where we won't be overheard through walls or by anyone who might be passing by."

Sienna fell silent, looking at me. That damn towel and those damn long hair were messing with my head. If I kept insisting, I'd give her anything she asked for, but I needed to be careful. I needed to make sure my emotions didn't overpower my reason.

"Go get dressed, Sienna. And eat. We don't have time to waste," I said more harshly than I wanted, because she was not at fault for anything, let alone for the insane thing I felt.

With that, I went into the room I had been using before she arrived, closed the door, and got under the shower, to cure the damn almost unhealthy desire I felt for that woman.

One day, maybe, she would be mine.

One day.

# CHAPTER SEVEN

## Sienna

A private jet took off from Louis Armstrong Airport in New Orleans just after noon. I watched as the things below grew smaller, wondering if that's how God saw me from the sky; as just another dot among so many others. Insignificant. Lost.

There was a time when I dedicated many hours of my days to prayers. I grew up as the good girl who went to church every Sunday because my family was extremely religious. I saw my brother recite the Lord's Prayer beside me, with his eyes closed, immersed in a faith I no longer felt when all those I prayed to stopped responding to me.

I wished I had the faith he had. But maybe things were better for him than for me.

"Are you okay?" Enrico's gentle voice pulled me out of my reverie, but I decided not to look at him, keeping my focus on the window beside me.

"This is the third time you've asked me that. I've flown before, you know?"

"I'm sure you understand that's not the intention behind the question."

I took a deep breath, trying to maintain the conviction that I needed to treat Enrico, at least initially, like I treated everyone else.

So, I turned my head towards him slowly. Every second I gained in that small delay was valuable to me because it helped me think about what to say to him.

I was used to lying. I was used to pretending, to playing a role. I was trained and raised to always smile, to always appear impeccable, and to only speak at the right moments. It was so ingrained in me that it was almost impossible to change, even for the man who had some power over my feelings.

"I'm fine," was my cold and direct response. My eyes probably glowed empty and emotionless.

Enrico was not the type of person who rolled his eyes or showed great reactions to anything. At that point, we were the same. I could swear there were many things happening inside him, but none of them would be evident in his expressions.

"I find it hard to believe, but I won't insist, Sienna. I won't drag anything out of you that you don't want to share. More than that, I won't force you to talk to me if you want to remain silent. As long as you're under my protection, you won't be obligated to anything."

"Under your protection?" I didn't want that phrase to have such an intense effect on me. I didn't want to feel my stomach twisting, much less my chest tightening upon hearing those words, said in such an intense way, like everything Enrico did.

"From this moment on, yes. I am taking responsibility for keeping you safe, but not just that. To also begin the investigation and prove your innocence, since that's what you chose."

Prove my innocence.

Return to the Cosa Nostra.

Was that really what I wanted? Could I simply throw all the truth in their faces and demand a life elsewhere because they owed me that?

It was a lot to think about, but apparently, I would have time.

We landed some time later in Los Angeles, and Enrico started moving around. He handed me a hoodie, which I quickly put on, hiding my hair, and did the same with sunglasses, which I also wore. Surrounded by security as we were, they might think I was a celebrity no one knew.

Everything seemed very prepared. We were guided to a car in the underground parking lot, and all the while I felt Enrico's hand either on my back or my arm, which made me wonder if he was afraid I would run away or if someone would take me from him.

Discreetly, I sighed in relief when we got into the car, and I was able to lower the hood. Besides, I looked back, realizing that we were being followed by the security guards who had escorted us.

"You're diverting a lot of resources for this mission. At some point, your family will notice."

"My money doesn't come solely from my family. I have my own. I have businesses that are just mine."

I raised an eyebrow in surprise, realizing that maybe I knew less about him than I had imagined. We talked a lot, whenever possible, but it had been several years since we had the chance, because Bruno was always watching me. When Enrico approached, when we spent a lot of time together, I was punished more and more.

I never forgot the first and only time I asked, with all the humility in the world, if I could negotiate my marriage with him because he was someone I liked.

I even shuddered thinking about the consequences.

The car took us along a road while I controlled myself not to ask anything. Still, I wouldn't be able to know where we were, considering we kept going farther and farther, to a completely remote location. Maybe it was even better not to know.

We got out after Enrico's armed men carefully inspected the entire area, and only then could I take a look around. There was a huge lake on one side and, on the other, a romantic-looking cabin, a considerable size with two floors, with absolutely nothing around.

The same men got back in their car and drove away, leaving us alone.

"Where are we?" I asked, abandoning my previous idea of not knowing the location.

"Running Springs."

The small town was over an hour from Los Angeles. A distance too small for my taste, but I had to believe that Enrico knew what he was doing.

"You'll have all the comfort possible, but I can't trust anyone being around you, not even a security guard. Do you think you can handle the house and the solitude?"

I looked around, taking a deep breath. There were animal sounds around; sounds I was unfamiliar with from living amidst the concrete jungle. Maybe crickets, or frogs...

There were also birds. There was the smell of earth, the sound of the water moving with the breeze.

It was the greatest peace I had ever known in my life.

"I can. I can handle all of this," I replied, feeling the wind tousling my hair. The sensation was so good that I closed my eyes.

"And with the idea of faking your own death?"

Enrico's question startled me to the point of almost jumping on my own feet. I would have done so if the shoes I was wearing weren't the same ones I had danced in at that club, since I hadn't had another pair to change into.

"What are you talking about?" I snapped, speaking louder than I should have.

"It's my plan. They won't look for a dead woman. With that, we'll be free to investigate the whole story, in your time, without fear."

"Enrico! They'll never fall for that story."

"They will if I do it right."

I was left speechless. He was taking the reins of everything, just as everyone had always done with my life.

No... that wasn't true. Enrico was asking for my permission, wanting my opinion. The fact was, I had always been so protected, so controlled, that I really didn't know what it would be like to start making all my own decisions.

Was this what I wanted? Undoubtedly, but what did I know about the world? At the first opportunity I had, I plunged into a sleazy club and would have been literally sold if he hadn't saved me.

An unlikely hero. The true Shadow Knight.

I was his charge from that moment on. Something told me he would make it his life's mission.

# CHAPTER EIGHT

## Sienna

The first step into the house almost took my breath away. I didn't remember all my conversations with Enrico, but I knew we had talked, at some point, about cabins by the lake as settings for the best romances.

Or rather... *I* had talked. He wasn't much of a reader.

But I could swear that our comments about it had happened when I was just a girl. Before my whole life was turned upside down.

How was it possible that he had remembered?

The decor of the place was made up of simple wooden furniture, but in a cozy way, as if he really wanted me to live in something more like a home.

He had told me that he was footing the entire bill with his own money and not with his family's fortune, but something told me that there was no need to economize. Enrico could have put me in a golden cage; a house or a penthouse worthy of a Hollywood setting, but he had hit the mark much more with his choice.

I could see myself walking through that house, making coffee, lying on the couch reading a book, or even cleaning the windows.

God... I even wanted to sweep and dust the furniture. I wanted normalcy. To be free, even within a prison.

"It's beautiful..." I commented, not showing half the enthusiasm I felt. Controlled, I took off my shoes and clasped my hands together, as if I needed to hold myself back from touching everything to believe it was real.

Enrico extended his hand wordlessly, and I took it, which led him to guide me to the stairs. Along with the dreamy, almost bucolic atmosphere, he seemed like the typical dark-haired hero with very blue eyes from romance novels. A gentleman, mysterious, intense, and protective.

The second floor of the house, where we arrived, was a kind of mezzanine, like a good romantic cabin. The ceiling was sloped, with a huge, comfortable bed near a window that looked out onto the surrounding greenery, creating a delightful environment. In the other corner, there was a bookshelf full of books, though there was still plenty of space.

I approached it, running my hand along the spines, unable to control myself.

"I haven't filled it up yet, so you can choose whatever you want. Just let me know what you prefer and I'll bring it."

I shot a glance at him over my shoulder with a half-smile.

It was, indeed, a prison, because I couldn't leave until there was proof of my innocence. Yet, he was making every effort to keep me comfortable and... happy.

If that word still had a place in my vocabulary.

We continued to tour the house, and there was a comfortable bathroom, with a sizable bathtub, another bedroom on the first floor, as well as a functional kitchen.

"I'm not sure if you'll feel comfortable here. If you prefer, I can look for another place and..."

Before he could finish speaking or I could respond, I felt something brush against my legs; a kind of fur, which made me lose all composure and let out a scream. Without thinking, I threw myself into Enrico's arms, clutching his shirt.

"What was that?" I asked, still terrified, and when I looked up, I saw that he was looking at me, seemingly surprised by my reaction.

His hands pressed firmly against my back, and I had the impression that he wouldn't let go anytime soon, especially as the little creature that had scared me earlier came back and stood beside us.

My heart literally stopped beating for a few moments.

Of all the things he had thoughtfully included in that setting, there was the most significant one. At our feet, brushing against our legs, was a tiny little thing.

I could barely describe the beauty of the animal, but it had a mix of dark brown and white fur, and its eyes were a blue very similar to Enrico's. It was an adult, and although I didn't know much about cats, I would say it was no more than two years old.

I crouched down, approaching it, and the little creature took a step back, somewhat wary of me.

I extended my hand carefully, feeling my eyes sting with the threat of tears.

I didn't want to cry, not at all, but it was impossible.

"I've always wanted to have a cat," I said softly, while still trying to interact with the little creature, even though it wasn't used to me yet.

"I know," he replied.

Of course, Enrico knew. He knew *everything* about me. Everything I had told him, he had remembered and paid attention to.

"Is it mine?"

"Yes. Of course. I thought you'd feel a little less alone with him."

I sighed, especially as the little scared one accepted my fingers on his cute face but ran away when I tried to pick him up, despite all my care.

"Does he have a name?"

"No. I found him a few days ago, before my trip to New Orleans."

"Can I choose one?"

"As I said, he's yours."

I stood up, as my new little friend had disappeared around the house, putting myself on my feet.

I wanted to kiss Enrico. I just wanted to press our lips together as a thank you, but I felt he didn't deserve that. He wasn't a pet, like the kitten he had given me, to receive gratitude or pats on the back for something good he had done.

Enrico was a man who needed to be loved. Even though, in the past, I had felt a crush on him, and he still stirred something in me, I wasn't a woman worth loving, because, just as my brother had always said, I was a frigid; the Ice Queen.

So, I simply extended my arm and touched him.

"Thank you."

With a nod, he acknowledged my thanks and then finished showing me the house.

We then gathered in the living room to discuss what would happen next.

I still felt reluctant about the idea of faking my own death, but that's basically what I was doing, right? I had disappeared, and theoretically, no one should know where to find me. The problem was figuring out how it would be done.

"We'll send photos of a body that could pass for yours. I'll forge a report, a medical opinion, and everything I can."

"You *can*? Is it *possible*?"

"Anything is possible when you have a lot of money."

I nodded once more, lowering my head, thoughtful.

"Things will be difficult, Sienna," he said again, with a firm tone. Even though I had always seen him as a restrained man with a soft voice and subtle movements, it was easy to feel the power he radiated. Observant, controlled, dark, full of secrets. He would make an amazing boss someday. "You'll have to stay here for a while, until we sort everything out."

"I've lived as a prisoner my whole life, Enrico. This will be the easiest part."

"You'll be alone most of the time. I'll come by whenever I can, but..."

"My fear is being accompanied. Fear of what people might do to me when they have the power to do so."

He frowned, narrowing his eyes, his gaze heavier than before.

"I will never harm you, Sienna. I would never hurt you. That's a promise I would die before breaking."

Our gazes locked for a few moments, in silence.

I believed in him. Believed in a way that scared me because it had been a long time since I had trusted anyone.

Enrico could be my salvation.

Or my complete ruin.

# CHAPTER NINE

## Enrico

The days were counted by the hours without Sienna and the hours with her. I didn't always manage to stay away from my family, making flimsy excuses for my absence, but things got worse when chaos ensued.

It started with a phone call at eleven-thirty at night.

I knew the nature of that kind of call, when it came out of the blue: either it was a tragedy or an urgent matter. Jobs that made me feel disgusted with myself, even though I was excellent at them.

Since I brought Sienna to that cabin, there had been no such intervention. At least not one I needed to be involved in. So I wondered what it would be like to face her after a torture session or a job that required me to get my hands dirtier than I would like?

On the other end of the line, however, I heard Alessio, my younger brother, greet me with a tearful voice.

He was usually more emotional than I was—perhaps a bit too much—but not to the point of shedding tears like this.

"Rico, *dove sei*?" "Where are you?" he asked, distressed.

It was the first time he had done this since I rescued Sienna. My father was the one who questioned my absences more, but always with a complacent smile when I made him believe there was a mistress involved. His phrase was always the same: "Have fun, *bambino*, but at some point, you'll need to find a wife."

Find her? She was there all the time... she just needed to accept me.

"What happened?" I asked, trying to avoid the question. Luckily for me, Alessio wasn't a gossip, and his state told me that what he had to say was more urgent than discovering what I was up to.

"Stefania, brother. I just got a call saying the car she was in had an accident. I need you here. I need you because... *Oh, Dio...* Our little sister, Rico... We have to identify the body. I can't do this alone."

I was a bit stunned by the news.

Silent, while listening to Alessio sob on the other end of the line, I felt a wave of dizziness and had to hold onto the nearest wall.

My sister. The sweet little one who was born so tiny, wrinkled, and crying, willful, but grew into a sweet, placid, well-mannered, elegant woman, a princess. She was the pride of us all.

I swallowed hard, controlling my breathing and my heartbeat.

Of course Alessio couldn't do it alone. I couldn't leave him, especially since I couldn't talk to our father, of course. I knew it wasn't fear that Massimo Preterotti would crumble at the news of his beautiful little girl being lost—if we indeed confirmed it was Stefania—but because he would be relentless even at that moment.

"I'll be there in an hour."

The drive, at a normal speed, would take an hour and a half, but I could put the pedal to the metal and cut that time.

I ended the call and jumped out of bed. I was staying in the downstairs room, so I allowed myself to at least sleep without a shirt. I didn't always spend the nights there, but when I did, it was hard to pull away from Sienna and think of her alone, unprotected, dealing with her own demons.

It hadn't been long since she was declared dead. I was with her when she received the news and made sure to observe each of her reactions. Of course, she was shaken, that first step we needed to take wasn't easy, but I also felt a bit of relief.

The next step for us was to make her talk about what she knew. Since we had gained a bit more time with the news of her fake death, I decided to grant her that right to silence, but at some point, we would need to talk. If the plan was, indeed, to prove her innocence, I would need to get some information, no matter how terrible the memories I had to access were.

And I could bet they were truly terrible.

At that moment, however, I would have to put those thoughts about Sienna aside because my brother needed me.

I put on some random clothes and went to her room, knocking on the door. I ended up opening it because it was an emergency, but I immediately regretted it when I touched it gently, intending to wake her, and Sienna jumped on the bed, startled, dragging herself across the mattress and huddling, using the comforter to cover herself up to her chin, as if she needed protection from me.

I needed to take a deep breath, not because of her fault. It was a defense mechanism, and I had invaded her space in a way I shouldn't have.

The cat's meow seemed to break the moment and make her say something.

Little Lestat. That was the name she had chosen for the kitten, which remained wary of me but already adored Sienna in a nearly possessive way.

"Enrico? I'm sorry... I..." She ran a hand through her red hair, brushing it away from her face. That same hand then went to her chest, at heart level, and I felt a bit more relieved and almost satisfied when she let go of the comforter, less defensive towards me.

"I'm the one who should apologize," I said, formally. "I didn't mean to wake you, but I need to leave. I don't know how long I'll be gone."

Her shoulders slumped. She had been there for about two weeks, and I had never failed to visit her for more than a few days. Three, at most, perhaps.

"What happened?"

"My sister. An accident... we don't know if..."

"Oh, my God!" she exclaimed, but in her restrained way, so much that even when she got out of bed, she did it with immense grace and almost calm, even with the world burning around her. She had been well-trained, and none of it was lost so easily. "I'm so sorry... I hope it's a mistake."

"I hope so too."

We went to the first floor, as she wanted to accompany me, and I stopped by the door, where there was a coat rack, grabbing my heavy coat and putting it on over my clothes.

"There's food for several days here. I won't leave you alone for that long..."

She nodded.

"Don't worry about it."

How could I not worry? That woman had come to depend on me for everything. If I disappeared, what would happen to her?

If I died...?

No, I didn't want to think about that.

Casting a look at her, I desperately wished we were just a couple, that I was going out for something trivial, and that I could lean in and kiss her.

Sienna seemed truly very vulnerable at that moment, like a girl. Without heels, I was at least twenty centimeters taller than her, and the pajamas I bought – along with all the other clothes she had in her attic wardrobe – made her look very innocent.

I pulled away before I did something foolish and headed to the place my brother indicated; a morgue.

Alessio was devastated and even more so when the person responsible for showing us the body lifted the sheet, and behind the deep bruises on her face, we recognized Stefania.

Despite being very close when we were children, I drifted away from Alessio over time. I envied him for not having undergone the same kind of initiation I did and for still retaining that carefree demeanor. For a while, I even hated him for being the second child, for having fewer responsibilities, for not carrying the burden of a legacy. An important future position in a dangerous organization that did not tolerate weaknesses.

Exactly for that reason, there he was crying, while I plunged into my own darkness.

All I could think about was that it wasn't an accident. Someone had caused my sister's death, so at some point, I would avenge her.

My tears wouldn't change anything at that moment. But the violence of my hands... that could make a difference.

It wouldn't take long.

# CHAPTER TEN

## Enrico

I had lost a sister, but everything happened fast enough for anyone to lose their mind as well. Considering that Stefania was betrothed to Dominic Ungaretti, the head of the Cosa Nostra in New York, and this union had the potential to protect our entire organization from extremist groups wanting to remove us from power, a desperate measure was taken.

Many years ago, when Alessio and I were still boys, our father married for the second time, after our mother's death, to a woman who wasn't from our world. He met her on a trip to Sicily, fell in love, and decided to go against all the rules.

We loved her like a mother, respected his choice, but that couldn't be said for the rest of the people around us. The marriage was viewed very poorly, and our stepmother, Cássia, was treated with much disdain by everyone.

This led her to ask for a divorce and make a deal with my father. He must have loved her a lot to allow her to leave for Brazil with our little sister Deanna, leaving everything behind.

I also knew that he fought a war to ensure that Cássia and Deanna were not pursued. I didn't know the details of the situation, because my father never wanted to involve us in any of it, but from that moment on, that sister had to return to our lives.

Stefania's body had barely cooled in the coffin, but a woman was to replace her at the altar.

All of this ended up distancing me a bit from Sienna. Deanna's arrival at our home was tumultuous, to say the least, as was Dominic's presence. Unlike the men in my family, disappearing with him around was a bit more complicated, as he was observant and very suspicious.

Fortunately for me, he was too busy being impressed by my sister.

I still went to the cabin to visit Sienna because she needed supplies, hygiene items, and I liked bringing her books since she was a voracious reader. Her little cat Lestat also needed food and other items, which forced me to always show up, but unfortunately, I spent very little time with her. An hour at most.

Even so, despite not showing my thoughts and not liking how things happened, having Deanna around was good. She had always been closer to Alessio, but I remembered her as a baby and being the first person in the world for whom my sense of protection became more pronounced.

Cássia had also returned, and we had our first family lunch with almost palpable tension. Not only between Dominic and Deanna, who would make their first appearance as a couple that night, but also because my father was a bundle of nerves. We all knew that my sister was not exactly a submissive woman, and unfortunately, the society we lived in was not very tolerant of rebellious women.

Still, I could almost say we were having pleasant moments. It was hard to see Stefania's place occupied by someone else, but I would be a hypocrite to claim that my late younger sister was a very significant presence at our lunches and dinners. I loved her, would have done anything to protect her, and still thought of avenging her because we all knew she was killed to prevent her from marrying Dominic, but she was quiet, well-behaved, very naive. Completely different from Deanna, who spoke her mind, ate what she wanted without caring about diets, and dressed in a completely different way.

The two couldn't be more opposite. And I swore that at some point she and Dominic would come to understand each other, not just because of the barbs they threw, provocative and full of malice, but also because of the way he looked at her when she came down, ready, coiffed, and in a beautiful dress.

"You look very beautiful, *sorellina*," Alessio said with a big smile, and Deanna just raised an eyebrow at him. She tried with all her might to remain indifferent to what he had done, but I knew it was a futile effort because she had to hide a smile when she heard him speak that way.

We all went out together, and I found myself next to her, walking towards the exit. Dominic had moved ahead a little to speak with his men, so it was just the two of us left behind, and I extended my hand for her to go in front, trying to act like a gentleman.

"Thank you," she said, rummaging in her purse. "Aren't you going to say I look beautiful too, Rico? It's your role as an older brother to make me feel flattered."

She was trying, no one could deny that. I had to give her some credit, considering that not many people tried to get close to me.

Or rather, they did try, but they didn't insist when they realized I had no interest in talking, reciprocating affection or courtesies. This happened mainly when it came to women.

One thing was falling into someone's bed – especially outside the world of the Cosa Nostra, on trips – because you needed to satisfy human needs; another was giving hope to young women with the intention of marrying the future head of Los Angeles.

"You look beautiful, Deanna," I said, which was true.

The subject could have ended there, since not only was I bad at pointless conversations, but also because I couldn't think of any topic to discuss with her.

That was until she turned to face me, a few steps ahead, and I saw what was holding her hair.

"It looks really nice on you," I said without much explanation, and I saw her look back at me over her shoulder, a bit confused.

"What?"

I pointed to the hairpin in her hair.

"I remember you coming to me crying because you wanted to wear it, but your mother wouldn't let you. I picked you up, put you on my lap, and you were inconsolable. You were always a chatterbox, so you talked, talked, talked, until you fell asleep on my chest."

"You took me to bed then."

I gave a nearly smile. The best I could manage, since it wasn't an art I had mastered.

"You were heavy for a three-year-old."

"You were a lanky thing yourself." Deanna was undoubtedly much more adept at smiling.

The memory of that scene tugged at my heart. It was the first time since her return that I allowed myself to open up to that kind of thing.

"I didn't remember that, Rico. Thank you." With a nod, I accepted her gratitude and we continued walking, while I kept my hands behind my back. "I'm very nervous about tonight. Thinking of us as children gave me a little more comfort."

"I'm glad I could help."

She remained silent, even stopping and placing her hand on my arm, forcing me to do the same.

"I talked to Alessio about it, but you know how he is... everything seems too pretty to his eyes, and I know he'd lie to make me feel better. You wouldn't."

"No. I wouldn't lie to you, *sorella*."

Deanna lowered her eyes, taking a deep breath and speaking in a tone of confession:

"Do you think Dominic will hurt me? Do you think I need to fear him?"

Serious, I looked into my sister's eyes, deciding how to give her the truth she seemed to want so much, but without making her even more scared than she already was, even though she didn't want to show it.

"Anyone should fear Dominic. But I don't think he'll hurt you. I believe you're safe, as safe as a Cosa Nostra wife can be."

What I wouldn't tell her was that I would kill Dominic with my own hands if I was wrong.

Still, she seemed satisfied with the answer. At least enough to nod and continue walking, especially when her fiancé and future husband approached, as the two would be going in the same car.

Alessio came up to me, hands in his pockets, watching the couple.

"How long until they kill each other?" he asked with a playful air that I wished I could match, but didn't fit with who I was.

"I truly hope they don't kill each other," was my much less witty but more concerned comment.

After we got into the car and settled in the back seat, with the driver preparing to leave, I sent a message to Sienna, realizing that I hadn't responded to the previous one I had sent about two hours ago.

**ENRICO:**
Is everything okay?
Please, let me know.

I took a deep breath as I put the phone back in my pocket, with a bad feeling that something was wrong.

I hoped it was just paranoia.

# CHAPTER ELEVEN

## Sienna

That morning started off rainy, and the day continued much the same way. It wasn't as if it changed much for me, considering that staying outside for long wasn't a prudent option. I would go out, read a bit by the lake, catch some sun, play with Lestat, but then return inside like the prisoner I was.

I wasn't complaining. To be honest, I enjoyed my routine. I liked getting up early, walking outside to exercise, having my coffee, and organizing things in what I had come to consider my home.

Was three weeks enough to turn a place into a home?

Enrico always encouraged me to ask for things to make the environment more to my liking, but I appreciated every detail just as it was. On days when I knew I wouldn't see him, I spent a lot of time in bed, lazily, and often read an entire novel in a single day. Not just the physical copies he brought me, but also the e-books I got on the e-reader he had gifted me.

I had internet access, which also made things a bit easier. I could watch movies, find recipes to try, and follow silly shows that I could never watch at home because Bruno found them too mundane for a "refined" girl like me.

My intention was always to avoid getting too attached to Enrico, but it was like Stockholm syndrome, even though he hadn't kidnapped me. My survival came from him, and he was my only source of human warmth during those endless days.

Often, I scared myself thinking if he was truly deceiving me and keeping me as his prisoner in that house because he was undeniably obsessed with me. But those were fleeting thoughts that came during somewhat depressive moments. I had access to everything. If I wanted to, I could escape. There was money for me in the house, and with the internet, it wouldn't be hard to hire a car from a company to pick me up. He himself had given me that direction in case of necessity.

Or maybe I was just trying to deceive myself... who could know?

The days were mostly the same. But on some of them, I woke up in good spirits and found things to do. I planted, started craft projects, and marathoned long series, finishing seasons in less than a week.

But there were darker days...

The problem was that there were ghosts inside me. There were memories that came up as very vivid scenes in my head. Most of the time, these were the days I dreamed of the things I went through, desperately wishing for someone to talk to, but finding myself alone, in the company of only Lestat, who had seen me cry more times than I could count.

And in moments when Enrico showed up, I hid that side of me and continued pretending to be the same Sienna.

He would tell me all the things that were happening, and I would converse as if I felt complete inside.

But it had been about three days since he last appeared.

I woke up feeling very, very bad on a Saturday. I didn't want to get out of bed and could have spent the entire day there, in fact. When he sent me a message, almost at night, I saw it but ignored it. I felt irrational anger.

It was him who had brought me to that place, and it was him who was leaving me alone. I felt a confusing mix of emotions. Hatred and gratitude. Anger and almost love. I swore that when he returned, I would shower him with slaps, losing my usual composure, but also kiss him and wrap my legs around his waist, asking him to show me that sex could also be something good.

If that would make him stay for good...

I was a chaos inside. So, to crown this feeling, I made the worst decision of all. I grabbed the bottles of alcohol that had been kept in the kitchen.

Enrico had decided to leave some there, in case I wanted to have a wine with lunch or dinner, knowing that I was never much of a fan of alcohol.

At that moment, it seemed I desperately needed it.

I started with a delicious red, but didn't take long to finish the bottle and move on to a white. I read Enrico's desperate messages and felt a terrible pleasure in each one. If I sent him just a "I'm fine," he would be at ease and stop looking for me. But at that moment, my most selfish side came to the surface, and I wished for him to feel desperate enough to run to me.

It was the fourth time in less than half an hour that he tried to reach me. He even called, but I decided not to answer. I was already drunk, of course.

When I threw the phone aside on the sofa, Lestat let out a meow. I looked at the little guy and realized he was staring at me in a very fixed way.

"Stop judging me or you won't get your treats." It was a lie. I spoiled that little rascal outrageously. If he whined asking for anything within my reach, I would give it to him.

He let out another meow, and I rolled my eyes because it was ridiculous to feel like the cat was talking to me and criticizing me.

Maybe it was indeed time to stop drinking.

But I didn't want to. Definitely not.

When I was almost starting the third bottle — having eaten very little all day — I moved to the window, thinking about the night outside. I glanced at the wall clock, which showed it was already past one in the morning.

The night wasn't as cold as usual, and I felt even more claustrophobic than before; which meant that the alcohol hadn't fulfilled its effect of numbing me and making me happier than usual.

Swimming, however, might be more satisfying.

What would it feel like to swim completely naked? There was no one around, no one would see me... Why hadn't I done it before?

Leaving the glass and the third bottle, already opened but still untouched, on the kitchen counter, along with the other two empty ones, I gestured for Lestat to stay where he was and headed for the door. I didn't even bother to take my phone, as it had been out of charge for some time. I just went, stripping off my clothes along the way and leaving them scattered on the grass.

It was quite dark outside, and the water looked like a black puddle of mud. I wasn't intimidated even then. I just went in, feeling my body slowly immerse.

When I felt the ripples that formed hitting the tips of my breasts, they hardened, and I shivered. I hated when that happened. I hated when my body gave signs that it might enjoy sex; of being stimulated.

I was nervous about touching myself; I had never considered masturbating. I didn't even know how I would do it. For me, it was impure to think about getting aroused, whether by someone else or alone.

But sometimes, just sometimes, I wondered about Enrico. Would he be able to change those opinions? Would I ever be able to free myself from that curse that followed me, with him being the one to break it?

I dived in headfirst, not caring how cold the water was, soaking my hair. The sensation was so wonderful that I almost forgot everything else.

I felt drunk enough to come back to the surface laughing, silly. Never in my entire life had I dared to dream of doing something so crazy, and yet it wasn't all that absurd. I was a twenty-five-year-old woman who had never tasted the real flavor of life.

I swore I would always be resigned, that I would accept anything if I could, at least, rid myself of Bruno. Even when I was promised to Giovanni Caccini, the head of the Chicago mafia, the option of marrying him seemed far better than living in the shadow of my brother, at the mercy of his cruelty. That was why I accepted the proposal, for sheer survival.

Not to mention that being a mafia woman, I could never refuse a marriage proposal.

My thoughts became tangled, and I could swear it had to do with the effect of the alcohol. Depression began to creep back in, and I didn't want to allow it. I needed to stay strong because I was in a much better situation than before.

I spread my arms and pushed back, floating.

I worked on my breathing, inhaling and exhaling, starting to calm down. The problem was that I was relaxing, relaxing, my head was getting light, and I had the impression that I was beginning to fall into an abyss. But before I let myself be carried away, I heard my name being called.

It was Enrico's voice. But it was obviously trapped in my thoughts; it was a daydream. An illusion.

My body became heavier. Heavier.

Falling.

Falling.

Falling...

Being carried away by the darkness.

I just wanted to sleep, without even remembering where I was.

# CHAPTER TWELVE

## Enrico

I slammed my foot on the accelerator like never before, speeding down the road and thanking my car for being a convertible that could reach almost two hundred miles per hour. I had to return home to get it after leaving the party abruptly without explaining anything to anyone, because I had arrived at the event with the family's chauffeur.

I arrived at the cabin, parked haphazardly, and entered the house through the back door, the closest to the garage, feeling extremely anxious.

"Sienna?" I called out, my voice loud, not even caring if she was asleep. I would hate to wake her, but I needed to know if she was okay and why she hadn't responded to any of my messages.

It didn't take me long to understand what was happening when I saw the bottles on the kitchen counter, along with a dirty glass.

Sienna had been drinking.

But where the hell was she?

Lestat followed me, and although he wasn't much of a fan, he started trailing behind, probably already guessing I was looking for his owner. Smart, he stopped in front of the cabin door, meowing loudly, drawing my attention.

I looked at the little guy, a bit suspiciously, but opened the door, hoping it might be a sign. Animals with a strong attachment to their owners could become protectors, right?

I saw Sienna's clothes scattered on the ground, creating a trail leading to the lake. Panties, bra, everything. She was definitely naked.

The outside of the house was dark enough that I had to squint to search for her.

The problem was that all I saw was a hand while the body was sinking.

She was drunk, in a lake, floating. Definitely not a good idea.

I took off my coat in a panic, as well as my shoes, while running towards the lake. I didn't care about removing any more clothing; saving her was more important.

I dove into the lake, reaching her as she was drifting further and further away. I grabbed her abruptly by the arms and pulled her up, holding her in my arms and realizing she was semi-conscious.

Her head hung back, and her long hair stretched out, still submerged in the water. I was scared, fearing she wouldn't be able to breathe.

"Sienna! Sienna!" I called out, in a desperation that could make my legs weak and disorient me if I didn't need to stay in control for her sake.

I carried her out of the lake, not paying any attention to her completely naked body, and laid her down on the grass. When I was about to start CPR, she opened her eyes.

She coughed a little, probably because water had gotten into her nose. Her gaze was lost, but she still seemed affected by the alcohol.

"Enrico? Are you really here?" Her whisper was almost choked, vulnerable, gasping.

I was ready to scold her, but that look and the desperate way she spoke melted me. Not to mention the question and the way it was asked, abandoning the stereotype of the cold, unshakable woman.

The fault was mine. How could I want to keep a woman safe but not think about her mental well-being, isolated in that place lost in the world, with only a cat and books for company?

Grumbling something, I reached for the overcoat I had left lying on the grass and wrapped her in it, lifting her off the ground in a rather undelicate burst.

"You don't need to do this. I can walk... I just fell asleep for a bit, I'm fine..." she said, still with that slightly lost and innocent tone, which made my chest tighten more and more.

But at the same time, I felt anger. Not at her, because I could never be angry with her. My problem was with the entire situation.

I used to need a lot of control to manage my negative feelings because they seemed to awaken something very, very bad inside me. They brought to the surface the worst memories that lived hidden and sheltered in my mind, and I knew that, if fed, they would have the power to make me explode.

I didn't even respond to her, but as we were about to climb the stairs, she called out to me again.

"Enrico, stop, please. I'm heavy."

She wasn't. What weighed was the certainty that underneath my coat, there was absolutely nothing. Sienna was completely naked, wet, and gloriously beautiful.

I let out another grunt and took her to the bathroom in the attic, setting her down on the marble stone of the bathtub.

"Take a shower," I said, sounding like an order, which was ridiculous because I wasn't there to command her. It wasn't my role. I didn't even have that right. Still, it was one of those cases where I couldn't control myself. "Get dressed and come back to the living room. We need to talk."

My behavior seemed to revive the old Sienna. Clinging to the coat, she lifted her chin, clenched her jaw, and looked at me with those glassy, cold eyes.

"Yes, sir," she said almost mechanically, but I could see the anger in her features.

That was good. I wanted Sienna to let loose; to yell, to express her anguish, to show her feelings. I knew I should be the last person in the world to want a reaction since I was also extremely closed off, but knowing how those bottled-up emotions suffocated me made me imagine how good it would be if she could let them out.

I could argue with her, complain, assert that she shouldn't feel that way, but I was tired too. The day had been crazy, with the whole event issue—something I hated because being surrounded by many people always made me very tense and uncomfortable—, with the desperation of not being able to reach her, with the insane speed of the drive, and then with the fear of seeing her in that lake, like that.

To think she could have died if I had arrived one or two minutes late? That made me nervous enough not even to run to the bathroom to take a shower myself. Even wet, with my hair dripping all over the house and my clothes soaked, I went to the kitchen counter, grabbed the bottle, and filled the same glass Sienna had drunk from, downing it quickly, wishing the drink were a bit stronger.

The cat made a graceful leap and jumped onto the counter, staying far enough away for what he thought would be his safety, but he kept watching me.

Somehow, if it hadn't been for him... maybe I would have taken longer to find Sienna and...

Oh, damn it! I was about to thank an animal. Talk to it! It was the kind of thing that woman made me do.

To be fair, I reached out and tried to pet him, and he even let me, but soon moved away, jumping off and continuing on his way.

I took another glass of the drink, still a bit hesitant to leave the spot in front of that door, but when I did, I decided it was better to go get our things outside.

I gathered my shoes, Sienna's clothes, smelling her scent in each piece. The white lace panties stood out among the others, and I had to clench my teeth to resist the urge to bring them to my nose. I didn't have the right to do that. Not while she hadn't opened up and given me a chance to truly have her.

I collected the clothes and put them in the dirty laundry basket next to the washing machine, and only then went to take a shower.

I ended up spending a bit more time than expected under the shower, pressing my forehead against the tiles and taking deep breaths, trying to push away the image of her sinking in that dark water... almost losing her.

Losing her...

She wasn't even mine to lose.

I punched the damn bathroom wall, feeling like an idiot for each of those bursts of childish behavior.

Stepping out of the shower, I dried off and dressed, returning to the living room, already expecting she might not be there after the long time it took me to show up.

But Sienna was indeed there. Curled up on the sofa, with the kitten at her feet, sleeping like a frightened child. Her long legs were curled up, and her arms were across her stomach as if she were hugging herself.

I watched her and felt my eyes grow heavy with compassion and... love.

God, how I loved her. How was it possible that the feeling was so much stronger than the determination to become indifferent to her presence?

I approached carefully and lifted her off the furniture, holding her as if she were porcelain. She stirred, pressing her head against my chest, and I feared she might wake up, but she merely sighed, and I had to swallow hard, feeling that she trusted me. Or the most she could trust in that situation.

"I'm here, my love. I'm here, I'll stay with you. I won't leave you alone..." I whispered, trying to calm her, and carried her to the bedroom, hoping she would have a peaceful night while I kept watch and protected her from anything that might harm her.

Even from herself.

## CHAPTER THIRTEEN

## Sienna

Something was tickling my nose. I brought my hand up to it, trying to ease the sensation, but it was persistent. I smiled, knowing exactly what and who it was.

"Let me sleep, Lestat," I said softly, in a fond tone.

My kitten, however, wasn't leaving me alone. For some reason, he wanted me to wake up. He usually wasn't this impatient, unless...

I opened my eyes suddenly, not just because of the thought that crossed my mind, but also because of the smell that greeted me.

Bacon... my stomach rumbled immediately. Along with that came one of the worst headaches I'd ever had.

I had drunk far more than at any other time in my life. I was definitely going to pay the price for my audacity. Besides... Enrico was home.

It was strange to think of it that way, as if it were his home or as if we lived together. "Home" gave me the feeling that we had a normal life, that we were a couple.

How crazy... We hadn't even kissed.

I placed one hand on my head, trying to recall more about the previous night. I remembered images of the lake, the desire to swim naked, the sensations, closing my eyes, and waking up in Enrico's arms.

I also remembered lying on the sofa, feeling so tired... so tired...

It was very hard for me to admit that Enrico's presence at home made me wake up feeling much better than the morning before, even with the hangover headache. And I also didn't want to smile at the sight of a glass of water and an aspirin on the bedside table.

I took them and slipped into the bathroom, splashing water on my face, changing clothes, and heading downstairs.

I breathed as I always did, holding back my feelings, but I couldn't help but marvel at the sight of that huge and dark man, with his hair tied in a samurai bun, wearing a black cotton shirt and jeans, barefoot, taking over the stove to make breakfast for me.

"Good morning," I greeted almost formally, sighing deeply in the most discreet way possible when he turned his eyes toward me.

They were so blue that even from the distance I was at, I could discern the shade of that morning, as it changed with his mood.

They were cerulean.

"How are you feeling?"

"A bit of a headache. Nothing I haven't experienced worse before."

I didn't want to sound too dramatic, but the effects of the previous night were still taking their toll. It wasn't something that would go away overnight. It was a process. Him being there relieved me a bit, because my mind was distracted, but I hated being so dependent.

"Sit down and eat. You'll feel better," he said in a tyrannical tone; the same one he used the night before.

I knew it was a trait of men like him, actually. But I also knew Enrico was a bit annoyed. Therefore, my intention was to tease, just that.

"Yes, sir."

I immediately regretted saying that because the crease in his forehead deepened, making him look even more tense.

"I'm not controlling you, Sienna. It's advice."

I wanted to say it was a joke, but I imagined Enrico wasn't very inclined to that. Not at that moment. Not that he was a fun person, but it was better not to poke the bear.

I did what he "advised," and we both sat down, starting to eat.

"It's good, thank you," I commented, and he just nodded.

His broad and muscular shoulders were tense, even while eating, which should have been a pleasurable act.

I chose to remain silent, letting only the sounds of our utensils and glasses fill the space.

That is, of course, until he decided to speak up.

He didn't look at me; he didn't raise his eyes, while his hand used the fork to stir his food.

"What happened yesterday..." He hesitated, as if searching for the right words to say. "How can I trust that you'll be okay in my absences?"

I understood what he meant. He wasn't glorifying himself or overestimating his importance to me, but shaken as I was by the embarrassment of being found in such an intimate situation—something I wasn't used to—I couldn't see things logically and rationally.

I straightened up with all my pride, lifting my chin, dropping my fork into my plate, ready for a fight.

"You have all my gratitude for giving me a chance to survive. *Grazie mille.*"

"Don't be sarcastic, Sienna. I came and found you completely drunk, nearly drowning in a lake at night. I'm almost afraid to ask, but what were you trying to do? Kill yourself?"

"It wasn't my intention..." I stood up from the chair because I no longer wanted to eat, and then lowered my voice to almost a whisper, not sure if I wanted him to hear me. "But it wouldn't have mattered if it had happened."

I was facing away from him, but I jumped and dropped the plate I was holding when a loud noise startled me. He had punched the table, hard enough to make me react.

"*Che cazzo*, Sienna!" he cursed, as the ceramic shattered on the floor. A piece of it bounced onto my foot, and I felt a cut, although the pain was muffled by the shock.

I had to hold onto the counter to avoid falling, as my legs gave out. I had little tolerance for shouts and outbursts like that, so I put my other hand on my chest, feeling my heart race. I could swear my eyes were wide, which made Enrico realize he had gone too far, and he apologized.

"*Scusami... Scarlatta, scusami.*"

I didn't want him to call me that nickname. It brought out feelings that reminded me of the innocent girl I once was. It didn't fit my emotions at that moment at all.

I saw him get up and come toward me, but I stepped back.

"Did you hurt yourself?" he asked, his cerulean eyes once again filled with intensity and compassion.

"It's nothing. I need to get the broom to..." I started to move away, but he stopped me, pulling me to the chair farthest from the mess we had made.

Enrico made me sit down and then knelt in front of me, resting on one knee, like a prince in a fairy tale, taking my foot with all the gentleness in his large hands, placing it on his thigh. He took a clean napkin from the table where we had been eating and began to clean the small wound.

"It's nothing," I repeated.

It really wasn't much. Like a paper cut. Despite my insistence, Enrico didn't listen.

When the blood was cleaned, he used his thumb to apply pressure to the curve of my foot, as if massaging it, which made me take a deeper breath and close my eyes.

Enrico seemed almost hypnotized, then began to use both hands, moving up a little on my ankle, making circular motions with his fingers, and I didn't know what his intention was, but his touches were *not just* relaxing.

A pressure between my legs manifested as he moved upward, and I bit my lower lip, wondering what would happen if he really climbed up to...

"*Scusami*. I shouldn't have spoken to you that way," he whispered with his soft, velvety voice, continuing to massage my foot.

I sighed again, shifting in my chair and even shivering.

"But I can't stand you saying it would be better if you died. I don't want you to think that, okay?"

As long as he continued doing that to my foot, looking at it without meeting my eyes, as if he were a servant pleasing me, I would be willing to say anything and agree with absolutely everything.

"Okay," I breathed out.

"I would have come for you, Sienna. Just like I did."

I opened my eyes, somewhat confused.

"Where?"

Enrico finally lifted his eyes to meet mine.

"Anywhere. Even hell. Like Orpheus and Eurydice, I would go there to rescue you if needed. If it meant bringing you back and keeping you safe, I would."

My head spun, and I was amazed by the intensity of his words.

What did that man feel for me? It was insane to imagine that someone could do so much and, until that moment, ask for nothing in return.

The problem was that if we continued like this, maybe... just maybe... I would start to be willing to open my heart, and that was extremely dangerous.

# CHAPTER FOURTEEN

## Enrico

From that moment on, Sienna seemed very quiet, even more than usual. I feared that what I had said might have affected her negatively. My words sounded like an obsession, and I couldn't pretend it wasn't real. The way I loved her wasn't healthy. Even if it only hurt me, because I didn't believe she would ever give me a chance, I didn't like the grandiosity of my feelings.

They hurt. And despite my great tolerance for pain, having been trained to endure injuries and torture sessions, when it came to that woman, I was nothing more than a coward.

We finished having breakfast, and she threw herself onto the couch with Lestat, while I stayed with the laptop on my lap, sitting in the nearby armchair, taking care of some emails, responding carefully since they concerned negotiations I was in charge of, not only for the *famiglia*, but also personal ones. However, I was interrupted by a call on my cell phone.

I put the laptop on the side table, stood up, and went outside to answer. Not that Sienna couldn't hear anything, but I was afraid she might make some noise, which could reveal our hideout and her presence.

"There's a limit to how much we can tolerate your disappearances at crucial moments, you know?" Alessio spat words almost like a curse from the other end of the line. The last time he called me like that, the news was that our sister had died. What could have happened this time?

"What happened?"

"Deanna was attacked yesterday."

My blood boiled instantly. At the same time, my whole body froze. I was caught in a ridiculous inertia.

"How is she?"

"Fine. She should be scared, but nothing shakes her." He paused, taking a deep breath before continuing, "We found her outside the party house, unconscious. Someone wanted to scare her. They actually want the wedding to be canceled."

"It's further proof that Stefania was killed."

"That's what I thought too."

We were silent, and I glanced over my shoulder, looking inside the house through the window, noticing that Sienna was watching me.

"Alessio... will you believe me if I promise I'm investigating something that might be related to this?"

He took a while to respond.

"Rico, you're my brother, and I would trust my life with you. Saying that your behavior has been strange would be redundant, because you're *always* strange. It's just that lately it's been a bit more so. I respect that, truly. I won't ask you; I'll assume you have your secrets, just like I may have mine, and you won't be pestering me about it. I just need to ask you not to let us down because I couldn't bear to lose another sister."

If my brother had been by my side, fist clenched, after punching me, I wouldn't have felt the blow as accurately. I couldn't have done anything for Stefania, undoubtedly, as we were caught off guard, but I had been so immersed in my search for Sienna, that would it have made a difference? Could I have saved her if I had been more attentive?

As I ended the call with my brother, I kept thinking about this, so much so that it took me a little longer to come back inside. When I did, Sienna was anxious, waiting for news.

I sat in the armchair, settling in while hesitating to tell her, but she needed to know everything. In some way, she would be my accomplice in this whole story and might be able to provide information to help me start somewhere.

And she realized this herself.

"I think it's time I tell you some things, isn't it?"

"Only what you want to tell."

She nodded, running her hand through her hair, letting it cascade like a waterfall after being brushed away from her face.

"I was very afraid of my brother." I looked at her hands, which were clasped in her lap, and Sienna started rubbing them together, visibly nervous. "He did things to me that..."

I placed one of my hands over hers while I listened to her forcing herself to stay strong, with a calm tone, letting the only sign of her nervousness be that little tic, which she probably thought was very imperceptible.

With my reaction, she lifted her head, looking at me with scared eyes.

"Don't force yourself. Don't torture yourself like that. Anyway, he can't hurt you anymore."

"But others can. Others who have hurt before."

My shoulders slumped as I looked at Sienna, starting to feel dizzy.

"Others?" My voice almost faltered.

"That's what I need to talk to you about. About a conversation I overheard through a door when they didn't know I was present. I should have told you before, but..." she couldn't finish the sentence.

"What did you hear, Sienna? You don't have to tell me details of what you went through, but if you can help... maybe my sister's life is at stake."

She lowered her eyes, embarrassed.

"You might have already lost a sister because of me..."

"No, not because of you."

"If I had said something before... But I swear I could never have imagined they would affect her. Just like I didn't know she would marry Dominic. But my brother was planning something with others. They held meetings at our house, talking about it. About weakening the five families one by one. His idea was for me to marry Giovanni to use me. The union of the Ungaretti with the Preterotti, undoubtedly, is a step they didn't foresee and could destroy everything."

"Who was with your brother?"

"I don't know."

I stood up from the armchair, moving closer to her and sitting down on the couch where she was. Lestat complained a bit, needing to jump to the side and even using his paw to scratch me, but I picked him up and gently placed him on the floor.

Sienna wasn't very comfortable with proximity, so I barely touched her. Especially with this subject, I needed to be more than cautious in handling her.

"What do you mean you don't know? Please, Sienna, I need you to talk. You can't be covering anyone up."

"Covering up?" she raised her voice a bit. "Do you think I would do that? With... with those..." She took a deep breath, trying to control herself. "Do you think I would side with them?"

She made a move to get up, but this time I needed to hold her back.

"Don't go, please. Stay and tell me what you know. Forgive me for suspecting, but I'm a bit tense."

Sienna seemed to acquiesce.

I saw her swallow hard and a kind of determination appeared in her eyes. Anger. Hatred.

"They raped me, Enrico. All of them. And still, I don't know their faces, except for my brother's, because I was bound and blindfolded the whole time. It was a dark and sadistic game... they..." Sienna lost her breath and seemed to give up speaking. Or simply couldn't continue.

At that moment, I simply didn't know what to do. What to say.

How to react to the confession of a woman who had been so hurt in that way?

It wasn't something I could pull from her memories. I could never make up for it. Nothing I did would be enough for Sienna to heal from that kind of suffering.

"They were very drunk. They didn't know I was home. Bruno had been abusing me for a while..."

"Your brother..."

"Yes. He thought he had the right, since we weren't really blood siblings. You know that story, don't you?" I nodded.

Bruno, Sienna's brother, had betrayed everyone, trying to kill the wife of the Chicago boss, whom he had kidnapped while she was pregnant. The accomplice in the whole crime was the couple's housekeeper, who we later discovered was the traitor's mother. He wasn't even the son of Sienna's father.

"He was the one who overheard and came after me. He managed to catch me on the stairs, threw me over his shoulder, and took me to the room, 'preparing' me, as he put it."

Sienna's hands began to tremble more.

"You don't have to tell, Sienna. Don't mention details."

"I won't. I... couldn't. But besides that, I overheard the conversation. I heard when they said they would start with the Caccini, targeting Giovanni. Then they would go after the Ungaretti. The Preterotti. The first three, then the others. Their focus was on you because you are the three strongest families."

"Did you ever know any names?"

"No. But I saw one of them. I saw when he arrived at the house, and also when he came back and looked for me... When..." Again, I felt her lose her breath.

It was painful to hear her speak those things and not be able to take a more passionate action. What I wanted was to pull her into my lap and hold her like a child, telling her everything would be alright. But I needed, at first, to keep myself sane to gather as much information as I could.

"I don't need details," I insisted, as it seemed too painful for her to open up in that way.

I was afraid of destroying her.

"Do you know what he looked like?" I asked, standing up and going to the living room rack, where I grabbed a pad of paper and a pencil. I had never drawn there, in that house, but at that moment it would be useful. "Can you describe him?"

"I think I c-could... but..."

"Please, Scarlatta. If it's painful for you, we can stop whenever you want, but if you give me enough information, we might be able to make a composite sketch."

Sienna was surprised but went along with me, providing precise details from her darkest memories.

By the end, I had a face.

Whoever he was, that drawing had become his sentence. Wherever he was, I would find him and kill him in the cruelest way possible.

# CHAPTER FIFTEEN

## Enrico

It was hard to leave Sienna behind after she made that confession. It was impossible not to look out the window as I got into the car and see her standing on the porch with Lestat in her lap, and not try to read between the lines to see if she was okay or if she was just continuing to struggle as she always had to be the woman she was trained to be.

I imagined that after letting all that out, she would be even more prone to episodes of depression, so unfortunately, I had to remove alcoholic beverages from her reach, but Sienna agreed to this. I couldn't go home, thinking of her getting drunk again and drowning in a lake or something of the sort.

Still, I knew that look on her face at the moment of farewell would haunt me for a long time.

But I had things to do. Not only because I had finally gotten some information, even if it was just a drawing that proved absolutely nothing and could only help me get to a name, but because it was impossible for me to stay away from the Cosa Nostra for more than two days before people started wanting to look for me. With Deanna's situation, even more so.

As soon as I returned home, I parked the car and headed straight to Deanna's room. I thought I would find a scared, traumatized woman, but I had underestimated my sweet little sister. She was furious, pacing back and forth.

"Are you okay?" I asked after she gave me permission to enter.

"No. He wants to control everything!" she snapped. "Wants to do everything his way. Wants to be my master. Wants to shove me into a damn plane to New York, as if it wasn't enough that they kidnapped me to marry me!" Deanna raged, furious.

"That's not quite what I asked," I insisted, approaching her as if trying to get close to a wild animal.

"No, it wasn't, but right now, it's the answer you're getting. I don't know how I feel about the threat, because it's not something that happens every day, you know? I still haven't processed it."

I gave up trying to get closer and continued speaking with her. I probably didn't have the right to insist, much less to meddle in her affairs, because Deanna and I weren't even close. No one could ever consider me a good person for advice or comforting words, and I wasn't even willing to try.

I was already leaving, almost passing through the door, when Deanna sighed and called my name:

"Rico..." I looked up at her, who was looking at me with a bit more sympathy. "Thank you for your concern."

All I could do was give her a nod and continue leaving before she noticed all the guilt I felt. If I had been at the party, would I have been able to keep an eye on her enough to prevent her from being attacked?

That would always be an unknown. How much my absences were affecting my family.

But how much was my absence affecting Sienna's life and safety? I probably meant more to her than to Deanna, who had a father, a fiancé, and another brother to protect her.

Thinking of Alessio, my next destination was his room, pulling the drawing from my pocket. I could ask my father something, who undoubtedly knew many more people and had more access to find the person in the drawing, but I didn't want to involve him.

Not that I wanted to involve my brother either, but he was a bit more harmless.

I almost bumped into him in the second-floor hallway, noticing he was very well-dressed and perfumed. A leather jacket, jeans, a black shirt, and his curls neatly styled.

The kid had always been vain, but I suspected he cared a bit more about his appearance when it came to a date.

And he had many.

"Going out?"

"Yes." He flashed a half-smile with a hint of mischief. "I met a *ragazza* yesterday. *Più bella!* She's a widow of a capo. Not even thirty. A body I'm definitely going to get lost in." Alessio brought two fingers together and kissed the tips as if he were talking about something delicious.

At least the woman was a widow. The problem was when he liked to seduce married women.

"Interesting to know you managed to get a date at an event where our sister was attacked." I had no right to judge him, but it was unavoidable.

"It was before. And besides, Deanna is fine. Dominic is like a wolf guarding her; she won't be in danger tonight, you can trust."

I began walking beside him as he headed for the stairs of the house.

"Do you have a minute?"

Alessio seemed surprised that I was interested in talking to him. To his credit, it had been a while since I had paid any attention to my brother. This time, again, it was for something of my interest.

But we were living in difficult times, and he had no idea how much.

"Sure."

"I'd like a bit of privacy."

"Let's go outside to my car."

I nodded and followed him.

We went to the house's garage, and Alessio unlocked the doors of his recently purchased Bugatti W16 Mistral, and we got in, with the top down, of course. Windows closed. Ready to share a secret.

With the drawing paper in hand, I unfolded it, and the first thing Alessio did was smile.

"You started drawing again?"

"Just occasionally."

"By the way, before anything else... I never asked you how you felt about her death."

I never doubted for a second that the subject would come up at some point; that someone would ask me about my feelings regarding the announcement of Sienna's murder.

The news had spread through the Cosa Nostra like wildfire. Some claimed she was killed by her own brother, others said that "a viper" must have made other enemies elsewhere, but no one knew the truth; that they were slandering, with their filthy mouths, a woman who had suffered far more than anyone would be willing to imagine.

"I'm fine," I replied tersely, hoping he would understand that I didn't want to continue discussing it.

But it was too much to expect my brother to have that kind of discernment and sense.

He reached out and placed one hand on my shoulder, with that overly emotional expression of his, which would seem very rehearsed if I didn't know him so well.

"I'm sorry, *fratello*. I know you loved her. But our hearts don't always choose the right path, do they?"

I clenched my fist in anger at the accusation about Sienna. If we didn't change the subject immediately, I would end up punching Alessio, and he wouldn't even know why.

"Can we focus on the drawing? It's someone from our circle. Do you recognize him?"

Alessio took the image in his hands, examining it carefully.

"This face looks familiar, but I think I've only seen it in passing. Maybe at a party or a meeting. The fact that he has that eyebrow piercing helps a bit..."

My brother was a source of hope for me because he knew a lot of people. As my father's capo, he was quite observant and a sort of "negotiator," mainly due to his friendly demeanor, charm, and ability to weigh things when necessary. People liked him – except for jealous husbands, since Alessio was the dream of most mafia women, known for his reputation as a lover and the beauty that was commented on by everyone – so we used his talent to soften those who could be softened.

If Alessio didn't recognize the person, it would be a bit more challenging to find out.

"The drawing might not be accurate either."

"From you? It's the most talented I've seen. — The compliment shouldn't flatter me, so I tried to ignore it, although it was nice to hear. — Anyway, I can try asking a few people. If you want, send me a photo of the image."

I needed to think. Involving Alessio was already risky, but having that drawing passed from hand to hand, from eye to eye, could lead to questions and eventually complicate things for Sienna.

"If I need to, I'll ask you. For now, I'll search on my own."

"What's going on, Enrico? I know you have this whole mysterious vibe, but you're starting to scare me. Who is this guy? Why make a drawing of him, almost a composite sketch? If he's done something to you, I'm your brother. Let's resolve it together."

And I knew he would be loyal to me under any circumstances. Even if I stopped to tell him about Sienna, Alessio would listen, weigh it, and give her the benefit of the doubt. The problem was that if we never proved her innocence and someone discovered she was alive, I would be judged as a traitor as well. I could save my family if they truly didn't know anything. Otherwise, I would bring them all down with me, and I couldn't allow that.

"I know you would. But right now, it's a situation I need to handle on my own."

I grabbed the car's door handle and jumped out, not giving Alessio a chance to say anything else. I slammed the door and walked away, heading back to the house while hiding the drawing in my pocket again, waiting for the moment it could be used and for when I would find the bastard who had harmed Sienna.

# CHAPTER SIXTEEN

## Enrico

"She's not coming," was the phrase Alessio kept saying, pacing back and forth as we both waited for Deanna to come down dressed as a bride so we could head to the church.

Cássia was much more relaxed, sitting on a sofa, looking beautiful in a blue dress, reading a book. As if she knew something we didn't.

"Of course she is," I replied, already irritated by Alessio's restlessness. "Brides are often late."

"Not this late."

"What do you know about brides?"

"What do *you* know?" He raised an eyebrow, his hands in his pockets, pausing for a few seconds just to look at me, but then he resumed his pacing.

I sighed, frustrated. To be honest, Deanna was taking a bit longer than expected, so it might be a good idea for someone to check on her and see what was going on.

Given *who* the bride was, she might have really jumped out of the window and run away, although I had a vague impression that there was some spark between her and Dominic.

Still, my father had gone up to fetch her. Unless he was searching for the runaway bride or Deanna had knocked him out to escape, I saw no reason for alarm.

But we were talking about Alessio, weren't we? The most passionate creature I knew.

"I'll check. I hope this will calm you down."

I didn't wait for my brother's response and went up the stairs, hands in pockets, trying to appear calm.

As I approached Deanna's room, I could hear a heated argument. She and my father were both agitated.

The argument was apparently about her dress...

I quickly understood the reason when I got close to the door, watching through the small opening.

The dress was red. A shade of blood.

"Spoiled woman? That's all you think of us, isn't it? We're hysterical, crazy, spoiled. I don't want to draw attention. I want to wear this damn dress because I don't feel like a bride, because I think it's beautiful, because my will has to prevail at some point in this wedding..." she said, defending her point of view with enormous intensity.

My lips curled into an inevitable smile because she was admirable. Even in heels, she remained so small, yet she was standing up to our father as if he were a lamb and not a dangerous mafia boss.

But she was still a woman. Still fragile, and as strong as a lioness – as Dominic had come to call her –, she was vulnerable to men who had no respect.

Unfortunately, my father was one of them.

I saw when he raised one hand, ready to slap her.

But I wasn't going to allow that, no way.

"Dad?" I tried to remain impassive as always, with no expression, not showing how pissed I was with the situation, but inside I felt my blood boiling. To avoid making things worse and acting on impulse, I decided to focus on my sister: "Are you ready, Deanna?"

"I am. Do you want to come in with me, Rico?"

The question surprised me, not only because Deanna offered but also because I actually wanted to accept. I imagined how proud I would be to walk her down the aisle, even if it was to deliver her into a marriage she didn't want, a marriage she was coerced into accepting.

But, of course, my father didn't allow it. With that settled, Deanna went out first, head held high, floating in her blood-red dress, while I stayed behind with my father.

"This girl... she's going to be the end of me. I swear to God..." I imagined he expected me to stay by his side, to make some comment about Deanna's audacity, but it only made me more enraged.

"I'm respecting you because you're my father," I started speaking very quietly, so Deanna wouldn't hear, "but if I find out that you raised your hand to her again or touched my sister with the intent to hurt her, I will lose that respect, and you'll have to deal with me."

I took the lead because I wasn't interested in hearing his response. There was no defense; if he tried to argue, things would only get worse.

I got into the car with Alessio, who also seemed shocked by Deanna's behavior and talked about it the entire way, probably not understanding why I was so angry. He might have thought I was pissed off at our sister.

We arrived at the church, and despite everything and everyone's astonishment, everything went smoothly. There were many guests, the ceremony was beautiful, and the reception overflowed with elegance, luxury, and ostentation, just as the Cosa Nostra liked. I kept thinking that everything would have been different if Stefania had been in Deanna's place. She was happy to marry Dominic because she found him young, handsome, and powerful. I had heard her talk to Alessio about how excited she was to be a wife, to have her own home, and to be the "queen" of New York.

She was completely different from Deanna. They had very opposite temperaments, which didn't stop me from having strong feelings for both of them.

So much so that, silently, when I picked up a glass of champagne, I lifted it slightly and turned my eyes to the sky, as a small tribute to

Stefania. As I took the first sip, I hoped she was at peace and that someday she would help us avenge her death.

It was when I lowered the glass, nearly empty, that I noticed a face that caught my attention.

It was a short man, but with a stocky build. He was almost bursting out of a tight suit, and his hair was shaved on the sides, fuller on top.

He was smiling openly as he was being served, like any other guest.

For some reason, my instincts were on high alert, and I had no doubt when I saw the eyebrow piercing.

He was the man who had assaulted Sienna and was colluding with her brother in a betrayal scheme that could put all of us at risk.

Of course, I had to think about the second part, which needed to be my focus, especially after overhearing what Sienna said about the betrayal plan and the things she knew. That alone would have been enough to get that son of a bitch on my radar. But imagining him laying hands on Sienna, against her will, violating her body, hurting and traumatizing her forever...

If I didn't control myself, I would have killed him right there.

But things didn't work like that. I needed to be sure it was him, get a name, gather as much information as possible. I could capture him, take him to a secluded place, and torture him until I was certain I was dealing with the right person.

Killing was no problem when you lived in the world I did. Killing an innocent? That was much more complicated.

"So, brother-in-law?" Dominic's voice reached me, always with that sarcastic tone that made him so distinctive.

I could never say I disliked him. But I also wasn't sure if I liked him, either. Dominic and I were very different, so we didn't mix much. Still, I believed he was better than many, for his loyalty and the way he defended our interests.

"Do you want me to congratulate you? Is that what you came for?" I asked, trying to sound sarcastic as well, though it wasn't my strong suit.

"I want you to wish me luck. Something tells me I'm going to need it with that woman." Dominic pointed to Deanna, who was dancing in her red dress next to Kiara.

"Take care of her," I said in a whisper, but loud enough for Dominic to hear.

He then looked my way, an eyebrow raised, a corner of his lips curved.

"Enrico Preterotti likes people?"

"Not people. I like *her*. I can be pretty violent when I want to, Dominic. I imagine you know that."

Dominic placed a hand on my shoulder, squeezing it. He was clearly a bit tipsy.

"Yes, I know. Good threat, by the way, but you won't need it."

"Great." I took my last sip of the drink and began to walk away.

I stayed alone for the rest of the party, glad that the time for single girls to come try to talk to me in hopes of being chosen had passed, but my desires lay elsewhere.

I gathered a few things, asking Deanna's permission, even though she didn't know who would receive the sweets I took.

When I got into the car and started it, all I could think about was how much I wished I had the chance to, one day, marry the woman I loved.

Maybe I was being sentimental, but I could indulge in a dream.

*I wanted* to indulge in it.

In the meantime, I just needed to keep her safe.

## CHAPTER SEVENTEEN

### Sienna

I didn't expect him to show up. Not on his sister's wedding day. That told me two things about Enrico. One: he was lonelier than anyone could imagine. Two: he truly preferred to be with me.

Often, my self-sabotaging thoughts tried to make me believe that all he felt for me was a sense of responsibility; that I had become a burden he needed to carry since he had brought me to that place and promised to protect me. But that lasted only as long as a breath.

Every time I caught myself thinking that way, I remembered the things he said to me, the way he looked at me, how every time he needed to touch me seemed to provoke him with the same sensation as if he were cruelly tortured.

Having him there, on that Saturday evening, just before dusk, was yet another proof of that. Hearing his car and seeing him jump through the window of my attic room gave me a thrill I shouldn't have felt.

So much so that when I stood up to prepare to welcome him, I had to take a deep breath and do my best to compose myself. He deserved the best of me, no doubt, but it was all I could give him.

Lestat also came, moving back and forth, hissing and curious. Still, he remained quiet as we both stood facing each other, staring.

Enrico was breathtaking. My Shadow Knight, with that prince-from-a-cursed-kingdom look. His long hair was swept to the side, as if he had just run his hand through it and messed it up in a very sexy way. His beautiful eyes were hidden behind sunglasses, probably because he had caught the setting sun on the road, and the tie he wore was loosened, hanging over his collar, on his white shirt.

It had been a while since I'd seen him in anything but black, and that lighter tone highlighted the nuances of his naturally tanned skin and the muscles hidden beneath the other clothes he wore.

"You can't go to the party, so you brought the party to you." He lifted a paper bag, and I could smell the treats coming from inside.

"I can't believe you stole snacks and sweets for me."

"For us."

I gave a restrained smile because I liked his response.

I liked it even more when he suggested we sit outside, like a picnic. It wasn't exactly something I expected from an idea of Enrico's, but maybe I needed all of it too much.

I saw that there was also a sketchbook among the things we took outside. With a different cover than the one he used for the police sketch, he certainly had it to use.

Enrico set up a campfire on the grass with impressive skill, and we sat down. I sighed with pleasure as I placed a delicious, flaky mini-croissant in my mouth, warm because we had heated it in the oven at home before we left.

I adjusted myself, sitting on a blanket we brought, propping myself on one elbow and lying on my side. Lestat was beside me as I watched the lake.

There wasn't much conversation with Enrico, as he was naturally a quiet man, yet it wasn't uncomfortable.

I closed my eyes when a gentle breeze caressed my face, tousling my hair, and I managed to open a slight smile.

Those were the moments when I realized that life was worth living. Just like I told Enrico that time, I never thought about suicide, even after everything I went through. Believing that I wouldn't be missed if I died was different, though I wasn't proud of it.

I still had some hunger for life inside me. Some small piece of my being desperately wanted to fight and find something that gave me hope. Something other than Enrico.

I didn't want to pin my survival on another person because I knew the kind of disappointments they could cause. No matter how much he was fighting to keep me safe, all that dedication could disappear and reveal a much darker side, especially since that man already had a tendency toward it.

When I opened my eyes minutes later, I saw that Enrico was focused, looking at the paper with the pencil between his fingers, drawing.

"Do I need to pose?" I asked, trying to control my curiosity.

"I could draw you with your eyes closed."

Once again, I almost lost my breath at that confident statement.

"Have you done this before?" Enrico looked up at me, very serious, and I bit my lower lip. "Sorry, am I bothering you...?"

"It's not that. It was your question. I thought you already knew that you've always been my greatest inspiration."

I brought my thumb to my mouth, biting the skin at the edge of my nail, looking for something to do with my hands.

"Can I see?"

"See what?"

"The previous drawings."

"I can't say no. They're yours."

Enrico shifted, signaling with his head for me to come closer, which was almost sweet. Indulgent. For a few moments, I forgot who I was, who *he* was, and just decided to enjoy the moment as if we were just a man and a woman getting to know each other better as adults, with a simpler future ahead.

I sat down beside him, pulling my legs up and hugging them, tilting my head toward him to look at the sketchbook.

He was incredibly talented. The lines were strong, defined, with well-executed shadows, contours, and proportions.

There were many drawings; not all were of me, but most of them were. I could find various versions of myself, from bucolic scenes among flowers and landscapes, at parties, in close-ups, full-body shots; none of them in compromising positions or nude. Not even with deep necklines or much of the body exposed.

All the drawings had dates, and they went back years, to when I was still someone within the Cosa Nostra. When most of the men I knew saw me as a body, as a piece of meat or an opportunity to turn me into a wife without opinions, ready to obey, he simply... saw me. He saw that there was a woman behind the image of perfection that was built at a very high cost.

I looked at him, my eyes stinging. With the feeling that I was about to start crying very soon, something I could never allow, because I didn't want to seem like a coward.

I didn't want him to see me as the fragile piece I appeared to be. I knew he was very protective, wanting to take care of me, but after what I told him, I wondered if we had taken several steps back; if he would become even more reticent toward me.

But what did I want from him? Did I just want a distant friend, a guardian, or something more...?

My heart had always been inclined to have feelings for Enrico, and lately, things had become more intense. Whether it was a real connection or just a product of enforced companionship, or my only cure for loneliness, I couldn't know while I was inside. At that moment, however, I wished to be more for him than just the damsel in distress he needed to save every day.

In a bold move, I took the sketchbook from his hand, along with the pencil he was using, placed them on the ground, one on top of the other, and shifted, sitting on his lap. If I were a bit more experienced, I would have positioned my legs, each on one side of his body, so we'd be facing each other. I would have taken the initiative in a more sensual way; I would have pressed our lips together less gently.

I would have provoked him to open his mouth and give me a real kiss.

But I wasn't dealing with a boy. I couldn't underestimate the power of a man who knew what he was doing.

I nearly lost my breath when his hands held me with immense firmness, one of his arms circling my thigh while the other positioned itself on my back, as if he wanted to hold me there.

He deepened the kiss, but in a way... In a way that made me melt immediately.

In a way that could have made me dissolve in his arms, even though I knew nothing about being loved in a real, passionate way. Even though I didn't know what it felt like to be touched by someone I *wanted* to touch me.

I had never even been kissed, but I imagined what it was like in theory, so when Enrico made our tongues meet, I had some idea of what it would be like, but I never suspected how intense it could be.

Enrico held me with fervor, growling with desire, while his mouth played with mine in various ways, biting my lip, sucking on it, and devouring me with such longing that I began to wonder if it would always be like this. If with every kiss he would incite me more and more to want... try more. To go further.

To places I never imagined I'd want to reach, after everything I'd been through.

When we pulled away, we were both panting, and I knew my eyes were burning with desire as much as his were when they looked at me.

"Don't do that, Sienna. I won't be able to keep controlling myself. I don't think you realize how crazy I am about you."

I was beginning to realize, yes.

"I don't want you to control yourself, Enrico, but I need you to know that I am a woman only halfway. Maybe I always will be."

"I want whatever you want to give me," he said in a passionate whisper that once again took my breath away.

"And what if I can never be your wife fully? If I can't ever?"

"Then I'll love you the same and touch you as far as you'll allow me to touch you."

And that's how I understood that I could never resist Enrico. Not even if I tried.

# CHAPTER EIGHTEEN

## Sienna

It was as if there were nails in my bed. I tossed and turned, reliving the kiss, despite my mission since it happened being to forget it.

At times, I was certain that allowing my heart to fall for Enrico was safe. Not that I imagined there was any salvation considering the girl I was always had some kind of feeling for him.

But when I thought it over... I started to weigh the cons against the pros.

Not because of him, but because of me. How could I want to tie a man to a woman like me? Broken, frigid, cold, with a reputation as a traitor? Everything about me was a trap, and although I knew Enrico wasn't the knight in shining armor starting to form in my mind, he didn't deserve so many problems.

But the kiss...

I had always thought that if I ever allowed myself to be kissed by someone, I would want the person to be gentle, to hold me with kindness, because I believed something rougher would remind me of my traumatic past.

But Enrico had been anything but gentle. The hunger he displayed while kissing me should have frightened me, but it left me burning inside.

And there I was, in bed, sweaty and feeling things I never thought I would.

I jumped up, startling Lestat, moving away from the bed and pressing my hand against a wall, feeling almost as if I needed to hold on to avoid collapsing, considering how weak my legs felt.

I wandered aimlessly, not even realizing I was wearing only a large cotton T-shirt that didn't reach mid-thigh. My hair must have been a mess, but I didn't care. I just wanted some air.

I went down the stairs, determined to get some fresh air outside, but a huge body sprawled on the sofa caught my attention.

For a moment, I thought he might also be unable to sleep, but as I approached, I realized he had fallen asleep right there, sitting. The laptop was on the table next to him, open, on an unfinished email.

In that state, he seemed much more real than the marble man I knew. His head tilted back, resting on the sofa's backrest, revealed his sculpted jawline and the pronounced Adam's apple. His mouth was beautiful. And experienced too, as I had discovered.

Enrico was drawn. With the same perfection those hands could capture images; his features seemed designed to create the appearance of a fallen angel. The way he wore his dark, longer hair, sometimes swept to the side; the way his body was shaped to show the strength he possessed, though not exaggerated, but with muscles in the right places, rigid and firm.

I sighed, still observing, feeling a bit hypnotized to the point of lifting my hand to try to touch him...

I just wanted to feel him a little.

But it was a mistake.

I barely managed to touch the tip of my finger to the spot where his beard began to grow when my wrist was grabbed. His movements were so fast I felt like I hadn't even blinked before I was thrown to the floor, with him on top of me, pinning my wrists against the carpet, our breaths ragged.

His eyes locked onto mine, first a little dazed, and I could sense the darkness in them, how shadowy they could become if merely provoked.

That position of dominance frightened me. The fact that his enormous hands had become like chains, pinning me to the floor, led to a sense of despair that took me back to the darkest times of my life.

He was a man, much larger than me, on top of me, immobilizing me and filled with violence in his thoughts.

I started to panic, and he seemed to notice.

In seconds, he began to come back to himself, looking confused.

"Shit...!" he growled, then made another swift movement, lifting me off the ground as if I weighed nothing, placing me on the sofa. "Scarlatta... what did I do? Did I hurt you?"

The poor guy looked terrified. He hadn't hurt me in any way. Something told me that even under the influence of hallucinogens, he wouldn't be able to do anything cruel to me.

Even knowing this, I couldn't control myself.

It was probably a mix of my reactions to the kiss, still being very shaken, and how abrupt his change in behavior was.

I didn't fear Enrico, but at that moment, he frightened me.

"Sienna? Talk to me!" He held my arms, and I realized my eyes must have been lost, even though I was looking at him.

Feeling suffocated, I tried to free myself and began to get up. Enrico held me, keeping me in place.

"Just let me go," I replied, standing firm but making a tremendous effort to do so. Even trembling, I lifted my chin and shoulders, though desperate to break free and reveal what I was feeling.

It was a sign of weakness. I couldn't.

"Stop it, Sienna!" Enrico shouted, but there was pleading in his eyes. "You don't need to act like this with me. You don't need to pretend. Tell me what you're feeling, damn it!"

Even he was losing control. Almost desperate.

What could I do? How could I stay firm when inside I felt myself melting, crumbling bit by bit?

My body began to tremble a bit more, and I struggled to free myself from his iron grip. Enrico gave me space, and I could have run to the bathroom, as that was my real desire. I even turned towards him, turning my back on the man, but I couldn't do it.

"What do you want from me, Enrico?" I asked quietly, keeping my back turned. "Do you want me to fall apart? To play the role of the fragile girl?"

"No. I want you to trust me to tell the truth, to not pretend."

I turned my body, finally facing him. I intended to remain impassive, but my eyes started to burn. My *body* began to burn. And it was no longer desire as before. It was anger.

"Do you want me to cry, to throw myself into your arms and lament everything? To lose my mind, break things, and mess up my hair?" I shouted. It had been so long since I had raised my voice like that that I didn't even remember what it felt like. "Do you want me to scream at the top of my lungs and say that I hate my life? That I just want to tear out the shit that lives in my head?" I even grabbed strands of my hair in my hands, completely out of control. "Is that what you wanted, Enrico? Was that your desire? To see my most human side? Well, here it is. Your muse is a fraud."

"Sienna..." He reached out, wanting to get closer, but I held up a finger, stopping him.

I couldn't say anything more. The tears were lodged in my throat like an impossible lump to swallow. I started to breathe heavily, gasping, then made the decision that seemed best at that moment. It was the cowardly choice, but I didn't care.

I fled, rushing up the stairs and into the bathroom, locking the door and leaning against it, sitting on the floor and waiting for the desperate tears I had let out to wash my soul, if that was even possible.

# CHAPTER NINETEEN

## Enrico

I was certain, seeing Sienna's reaction, that I had ruined everything. With a single move, an unexpected reaction, I wasn't even fully conscious to truly blame myself.

It had been an impulse. Being abruptly woken up by suspicious noises in the middle of the night made my body react like the warrior I had been trained to be. Fortunately, I wasn't armed.

Not that I would have started shooting, but if I had reached for the holster and aimed the revolver at Sienna, I would never forgive myself.

I had sworn that we were making some progress, especially after she took the initiative with the kiss. I thought about it for hours, so much that I couldn't even concentrate on work-related tasks that were pending. Not even to send the email to the trusted person I intended to hire to investigate the guy I saw at Deanna and Dominic's wedding.

I ended up crashing like a stone, thinking about Sienna's body finally molding to mine, the sensation of my hands touching hers, and my mouth meeting hers.

When I woke up, there she was, beneath me, subdued, but not in the way I wanted.

She was terrified, undoubtedly recalling the moments when she had been abused.

What could I do to change that?

I kept thinking, dreading leaving her alone, but certain that there might be a way to help her let go a little more. Of course, it was very painful to see her like that, tormented, screaming and crying, but it was better than imagining her suppressing a passionate reaction and keeping all those demons inside.

I took the car and went out, but not too far. Although the cabin was in a very remote area, there was a town at least half an hour away, and I found a 24-hour store that had what I needed: alcohol.

I didn't find the quality wines like the ones Sienna drank the day she got drunk, but I got a few things that would work.

Upon returning to the house, I was greeted by Lestat, who looked at me with those eyes that seemed to judge me all the time, and I felt a bit lost. I feared that Sienna had done something foolish again, but I saw light under the crack of the bathroom door in her room, confirming she was still there.

So I knocked.

"Please come out. I brought alcohol. Come get drunk again if that makes you feel better."

Sienna didn't respond, but I waited, especially when I started hearing movement from inside.

With very red eyes, she opened the door, just a crack, lifting her head to look at me.

"Are you going to *let* me drink?" Okay, I preferred the sarcasm over the fear. I could deal with that.

"Let's drink together, safely, without either of us doing something foolish. We'll take care of each other."

Sienna agreed, hesitantly. To be honest, the idea of both of us getting drunk after that earlier kiss started to seem quite dangerous, but I intended to stay sober enough not to make mistakes that could have consequences.

In a few moments, we were on the porch of the house, with two glasses of a drink that made Sienna cough after downing the whole glass at once.

"Yuck, this is horrible," she commented, holding her chest. "Give me more."

I managed a restrained smile, pouring her a bit more, and I took a sip myself, making a face.

We both sat in silence, watching the lake and witnessing the dawn unfold before our eyes, somber and mysterious, just like our souls.

"Why are you called the Shadow Knight?" I was surprised by the question, so much that I gave her a narrow look, curious. But Sienna raised her hand, sort of trying to explain herself. "I get it. It suits you, to be honest. But how did it start?"

"Alessio, of course. Who else?"

She shook her head.

"That makes sense. But I never knew when it started happening. You used to be... different. Just like me. You already know what happened to me, what turned the switch. What happened to *you*?"

I shifted in my seat, uncomfortable, grunting and drinking more of that awful stuff.

"It's not a pretty story."

"Neither is mine. But I've already confessed to you what happened to me. I won't force you if you don't want to access the memories, but I won't judge you for anything."

I knew that. And it wasn't a matter of leaving the memories dormant, because they were always there. The problem was telling *her*. Still, I wouldn't underestimate her ability to handle things.

"I was taken to a shed. They pulled me out of my bed in the middle of the night, with no explanation, with no idea of what was happening. I was tied up, with no food and only water, naked, in the cold, pissing on myself. Religiously, morning, noon, and night, they would throw a bucket of ice-cold water on me, which was almost like dying. Painful, terrible. But they also beat me, whipped me, burned me, and cut me."

"What was the point of that?"

"They wanted me to learn to get out of situations like that. On my own. But I was just a kid."

"Yes, you were," she whispered, pitying me.

"When I could no longer endure the hunger and thirst, they let me go. I was taken to a bed, in the same shed, clothed, fed, and I swore the nightmare was over. As soon as I recovered, they started again. My father would show up occasionally and yell at me that this was not how a man behaved, that he was disappointed."

"How did it end?"

"When I pretended to faint and was released. For a few seconds, I had my freedom back. I killed two of them. With my hands. I broke their necks and watched as they pointed guns at me, but my father didn't let them hurt me. At that moment, I was nothing more than an animal."

"It was survival."

"Yes, I know. But it didn't end there. There was more time for other kinds of training. Pain tolerance, for example. I spent days enduring different forms of torture because my father thought it would make me a stronger boss when the time came. When it was all over, I couldn't return to what I was before. I was already lost."

Sienna's face was a mask of compassion. I didn't want that, not from her, but I understood that it was the kind of thing that was told and would be impossible to ignore.

I poured myself another drink, took a big gulp, and swallowed, already starting to not feel the horrible, bitter taste.

"That's when I became who I am today. I trained to be the best warrior I could be because I couldn't bear to be put in a situation like that again without knowing how to fight, without knowing how to defend myself."

Sienna bit her lower lip, thoughtful.

We continued drinking for a while longer. Sienna had two more glasses, while I was still on my second, slowly. Suddenly, she stood up, positioned herself in front of me, and stretched out her hand.

"Can you give me your phone?"

"What do you want?"

"Some music."

"I don't have an app for that... I don't listen to music."

She raised an eyebrow, persistent. Sighing, I handed over the device and watched her fiddle with it.

"I'm not going to look at your messages with girls, Shadow Knight, don't worry."

"There are no girls for me, Sienna. There is only one."

I noticed she became a bit too serious, looking at me for a few seconds, as she always did when I gave her too intense an answer.

She looked down at the phone again and finally, music started playing from it. An old jazz tune, with a sensual beat.

She snatched the bottle from my hand and went inside the house, signaling for me to follow. I stood up, trailing after her because it was my fate: to chase after that woman, wherever she went.

She placed the phone on the kitchen counter and sat on the dining table, still holding the bottle. She stood on top of the wooden surface and began to dance.

"I've never done anything like this, Enrico. That day I swam naked in the lake was just a little madness. I think we can indulge in one more today... Come with me."

She started to move; at first timidly, but gradually loosening up, swaying her hips slowly, bringing the bottle to her mouth, drinking straight from the neck.

She was wearing only a loose cotton shirt, much larger than her, but it rose as she lifted her arms.

The music grew more intense, as the beat increased, and Sienna tossed her hair to the side, twirling her head, which left me hypnotized.

"I've danced for some horrible men, you know? It's nice to dance for one who sees me as more than just a body. You don't just think I'm *pretty*, do you, Enrico?"

Sienna was teasing. But again, I preferred those versions of her, especially the looser and less restrained ones, less imprisoned by themselves.

"No, *Scarlatta*. I *love* you."

Maybe I was also a bit affected by the drink because it was the first time I confessed my feelings in that way. But there was no point in hiding them, especially since I was always willing to show them. At that moment, after she had let so much of herself come to the surface, I felt the need to make her understand how loved she was. That I was willing to do anything for her.

Sienna looked at me a bit confused. Not surprised, because she probably already knew, but she stopped dancing. I condemned myself for having said something that prevented her from continuing to let go, to express herself.

I felt even worse when she began to cry.

"I'm sorry, Rico. I'm sorry... I'm too sensitive today. I'm not like this... I'm not... it's just..." Sienna brought one hand to her face, starting to tremble again, so I took the bottle from her hand, placing it on the kitchen counter near the phone. I returned to her, lifting her off the table and holding her in my lap, as if she were a frightened child.

With desperate hands, she clung to my shirt, resting her head on my chest, sobbing. It was perhaps the first time she allowed herself to do that in front of me.

"Why has life been so cruel to us, Rico? Why? Why didn't they let us be together, even within the damn Cosa Nostra? Why did they treat you like that? Why did they hurt me *so much*?"

I barely knew what to do with her at that moment. All I could do was hold her close and let her cry, taking advantage of the fact that she was opening her heart.

I carried her up the stairs, into her room, and laid her on the bed. Without the courage to leave her alone, I simply lay down next to her, pulling her close and hugging her, kissing the top of her head, letting her cry and cry, for a long, long time.

Until she fell asleep in my arms, looking like a tormented angel, while I watched over her, kept vigil, and stroked her hair, ready in case she needed me at any moment.

# CHAPTER TWENTY

## Sienna

I woke up still accompanied in bed, almost surprised that Enrico remained by my side. As soon as I shifted a bit, showing that I was waking up, he opened his cerulean eyes and looked at me with that love I didn't know until he saved me in every possible way.

"Good morning," I greeted him, thinking about how intimate that moment was. How personal it was to wake up next to someone.

"Good morning, *Scarlatta*."

I had to also think about how sensual that word sounded whispered with a slight morning rasp.

"I spent the whole night thinking about what I told you about my initiation," he continued.

"I'm sorry. I shouldn't have made you think about all that."

"It wasn't that. But because I think what helped me get through it was the training I underwent. The way I strengthened myself, how I learned to use weapons, how I learned to fight."

"You got over it?" I asked, surprised.

"No. Maybe the word sounded wrong. These days I'm not afraid. I can't control what happens outside. At some point, I might be captured, especially considering there's an impending war, from everything you've told me. I might be tortured again and relive all that shit from the past. But today, I'm more prepared for it."

"And what do you mean by that?"

"That I think I need to teach you a thing or two about defending yourself."

I took a deep breath, almost happy with his decision. If there was one thing I hated about my brother, besides all the horrible things he did to me, it was the certainty that he wanted me to stay defenseless, not knowing how to protect myself, because he didn't want me to use anything I learned against him.

That day, therefore, Enrico began training me, as he had promised. We started with some self-defense, which was what we could do at the moment, with what we had.

He was big and heavy for me, so I ended up on the ground many times, which triggered many things, but I kept standing firm. It was such a full day, where I spent so many hours moving, that I fell into bed at night, without dreams, without nightmares, and was awakened very early the next morning.

Enrico stayed with me for three days, training me, until he needed to return. During his absence, he left me physical exercises to do, to work on the strength of my arms and legs. Without even knowing it, he was not only helping me gain a bit of confidence to protect myself but also saving my days from loneliness, as I could fill them with something. Besides knowing that physical activity produced serotonin and helped with depressive feelings and loneliness.

When he returned, shortly after, he started teaching me how to shoot, gifting me with a firearm, and also made me learn how to throw and use knives for self-defense, how to hold them, how to move them.

He pushed me hard, not sparing me. When I was tired, he only gave me a few minutes to rest, drink water, and we would return. He said we were against the clock because we never knew when something would happen.

Even though we were taking this training seriously, things got hot very quickly, to the point of scaring me. Just like it happened with my first and only kiss with him, I swore I would be the type of woman who appreciated slower and more delicate things, but when Enrico wrapped his arms around me, holding me roughly in self-defense work, for a few moments, I had to force myself to fight and free myself from his embrace.

Most of the time, I felt that he also suffered from the closeness.

In one of our sessions, outside the house, his role was to act as the attacker, grabbing me from behind and bringing me to the ground. My role was to free myself from him as quickly as possible and keep Enrico away from me, either by immobilizing him or fleeing. As I became stronger and more resistant, he made it harder, almost like levels in a video game.

From the beginning, I knew he was taking it easy on me. I didn't know much about Enrico's skills, but I heard rumors that he was lethal, very strong, and experienced. That anyone who fell into his hands, whether a traitor or with bad intentions, would have a very grim fate.

People exaggerated, invented, and lied. They liked to create even heavier stories when there was something terrifying about them. Especially when talking about a ridiculously handsome man with that dark appearance. That was supposed to scare the starry-eyed girls, but it attracted them like moths to a flame.

That day, he was particularly challenging. I knew things were a bit complicated regarding Deanna, as she had been receiving threats, so that was also weighing on his mind. He was also investigating someone he discovered to be called Fredericco Bonia, the guy with the piercing I described to him and saw at my sister's wedding. Even though I already knew who he was, he wanted something to prove it was the one who hurt me before going against an innocent person.

He ended up taking it out on me.

We were repeating the same self-defense exercise after doing a running session around the lake. He would also have me swim sometimes, which contributed to building my endurance.

But things weren't easy this time.

He held me with more force, and I had to fight with more determination. He would knock me down just for me to get up again, and I knew that all this was not only a trick to make me stronger but also to face my fears. Of course, I didn't fear Enrico, I knew he wouldn't hurt me, but after the day I panicked with his passionate reaction to knocking me to the ground and immobilizing me, we were making progress.

It was a struggle until I managed to catch him off guard and bring him to the ground. I mounted his hips and grabbed his wrists, pinning him to the floor, smiling, breathless.

For a few moments, I was so happy with my small victory that I didn't even notice the look Enrico gave me.

He was my captive at that moment—or at least I thought he was, because I knew he could free himself from my hands very quickly—and I should do something about it.

Since the first time I kissed him, I learned that Enrico wouldn't take any initiative regarding me, not because he wasn't a man of action, but because I had my traumas. If I wanted him, I would have to take him.

I leaned toward him, letting my ponytail fall over my shoulder. I was about to kiss him, bringing my lips close to his, but I couldn't even touch them because Enrico easily freed himself from my hands, wrapping his arms around me, arching his head to reach the distance I maintained because I didn't know how to assert myself.

The sensation was the same as the other time. A whirlwind of crazy emotions because I didn't know that way of being touched. I didn't know the contact of a man who wanted not only to extract pleasure from me but to reciprocate it.

Enrico spun us around and positioned himself on top of me, using one arm to support his body and not hurt me. My arms ended up around his shoulders, as if I needed to cling to a lifeboat before being completely drowned in my own confusions.

One of Enrico's hands slipped under my shirt, and he squeezed my waist while letting out a growl against my mouth. Controlling himself, restraining himself. For me. He was denying his own desire, even though he seemed almost wild, to preserve me.

Despite that, his tongue didn't spare me, diving into my mouth and demanding, dancing voraciously with mine, making me gasp. When he let his lips start descending down my neck, my fingers grabbed his hair, which was tied in a bun, and let it fall like a curtain. The tips were wet with sweat, brushing against my skin, especially because I was wearing a lycra top that left my chest and shoulders exposed.

Then Enrico moved a little further down, reaching my stomach. He used his tongue to kiss me there, circling my belly button with its tip, and his hand closed into a claw before touching my breast.

I took it and placed it there, wanting to feel the sensation.

The friction of his finger with the fabric, which consequently covered my nipple, made my head spin, and I opened my mouth to let out a moan. Shy, almost a purr, which surprised me.

I immediately brought both hands to my mouth, completely dismayed, because I didn't expect to react that way to something related to sex. Enrico also seemed surprised, as he pulled away, stopping his kisses, hovering over me and looking at me with a furrowed brow.

"Am I going too far?" he asked, still with that whisper that left me dizzy as much as his kisses.

I should say yes. I should push him away and set a limit. I should preserve myself.

But that's not what I replied to him.

"Show me? Show me what it's like...?" I said hesitantly, almost scared.

"What? What do you want me to show you?"

"What it's like to feel pleasure. What it's like to *enjoy*... sex."

Enrico's chest rose and fell with a deep breath. His gaze fell on mine with that expression that made me realize he had all his attention on me. All his attention on my sudden request.

"Are you sure?"

"I am. I... want to know. I want... to be whole again. For you."

"You already are."

"Then I want to be whole for *myself*."

Enrico nodded, and I understood that this was a decision with no turning back. But it could mean everything and nothing.

All I wanted was to heal.

# CHAPTER TWENTY-ONE

## Enrico

I definitely didn't expect it. Not even in my wildest dreams could I have imagined that our lesson that afternoon would end in kisses, much less with Sienna asking me to take her to bed.

And I was a bit lost.

Damn... and how could I not be? For starters, she was the woman I had been completely crazy about for many years. The woman I had sworn for a long time would become my wife because it made sense, considering the importance of our families within the Cosa Nostra.

The woman who had been taken from me and became forbidden, who I lost more than once – both when she was promised in marriage to someone else and when she was accused of betrayal – but who was finally in front of me, in an almost romantic setting, with a lake surrounding us and a lot of privacy.

But she had become a challenge for me. Not just because the desire I felt was so absurd and intense it could leave me vulnerable in her hands, but also because I wanted the experience to be the best it could be. I wanted to be the best lover, so her body would accept and receive me with the surrender she deserved.

I stood there for a while, just contemplating the stunning woman who would be mine.

Her hair was tied in a loose ponytail but somewhat messy from the activities we had done. There was no makeup on her face, but she still looked like porcelain, the picture of perfection.

I reached out, letting the red strands fall loose, like waves from a calm sea, framing her features. Sienna was breathing steadily, but I felt her lower lip tremble when she took a step forward.

"We don't have to go any further, *Scarlatta*."

"We do. *I* need to."

I then pulled her towards me and kissed her. I pressed our lips together once more, first softly, just allowing the contact and letting our tongues meet, in the way I had noticed she liked. I was a bit gentler, wanting to seduce rather than devour, bringing one hand to her face, holding it, while the other went straight to her hip, pulling her against me.

I noticed she held her breath when she felt my erection against her. I always reacted that way to her, but it was the first time I didn't try to hide it, afraid of scaring her.

I held the other side of her face as well, using my thumb to caress it, taking as much time as possible kissing her. I believed her mouth wouldn't fully satisfy me, but it would certainly calm my body from that uncontrollable desire.

Or so I thought. But as I heard the sounds I was making and felt her body moving against mine, it was impossible to keep control.

I was a ticking time bomb at that moment.

I didn't want to take her roughly, at least not the first time. I needed to find a way to make my body stop burning, stop aching.

With as much gentleness as my rough hands, amidst the frenzy, could manage, I started removing her clothes, leaving her naked. I did the same with my shirt, leaving only my pants, keeping my eyes on her, and observing Sienna's reactions as a part of me became exposed.

I had scars, and she saw them. They were mostly marks from my initiation. But there was also one from a knife wound I received during a job. Another from a gunshot to my shoulder. A fourth from something else I didn't remember. A fifth from a knife cut.

They were pieces of the violence that lived in me. From the fights I had been in.

I also looked at her. Although I had seen her like this before, it was the first time I had the right to look at her; that I didn't feel like one of those bastards who devoured her with their eyes, objectifying her.

I didn't want just to look. I wanted to touch her bit by bit, feel the texture of her skin on the tips of my fingers; I wanted to place my mouth on every part of her body, from feet to head.

My true desire was to lay her down on that grass and sink into her so deeply that no one would know where we began and ended. I wanted to dissolve inside her, find and lose myself.

But I needed to be calm.

I crouched a little and held her by the thighs, placing her legs wrapped around my waist, which made her let out a surprised squeal. Needing to calm down a bit more, I started taking her towards the lake, entering with her slowly, so she wouldn't feel the shock of the temperature.

"What... What's going on? I thought you were going to take me to the bedroom..."

"Later. We can start right here."

"We can?" Her innocence fascinated and scared me at the same time. She had already experienced sex, but in the worst possible way, so she didn't know anything about different ways of experiencing pleasure.

"Yes. We're not in a hurry. First, I want to teach you how to pleasure yourself."

She seemed surprised, even to the point of being speechless.

"I never..." She didn't finish the sentence, looking very embarrassed.

"Never touched yourself?"

"No. Never... I..."

Before she could finish speaking, I lifted her a bit higher in my arms, keeping her in the same position, supporting her on the edge. One of my hands I used to take hers and guide it between her legs, through our bodies, holding her thumb and making it move in circles, massaging her clitoris.

She shivered at the first sensation, so I guided her other finger, the middle one, to use it to penetrate herself.

"Go as deep as you can, darling."

"I..." Sienna hesitated, but eventually did what I asked. But the moment she felt something entering her body, she tensed up so much I thought she was going to collapse. "I can't, Enrico... I can't."

"You can. It's you touching yourself, darling. Not me." I raised her hand to show her; if she got into a loop of anxiety and panic, she might start getting confused.

With that suggestion, she nodded.

"Go deeper and move your finger. Try to find the most pleasurable spot for yourself."

She was lost, so I started helping her, guiding her hand to find a rhythm. To help her relax, I lowered my mouth to one of her breasts, licking a nipple, testing. When I heard her gasp, I dove even deeper, sucking it hard, making her moan. While I attended to that generous part of her body, I continued helping her masturbate, encouraging her to increase the pace, urging her to move her finger in and out, faster and faster.

"Enrico!" Her name came out in a moan, and I had to pull her hand away, grabbing a clump of earth around the lake with my free hand to keep control.

"Are you okay?"

"I don't know..."

I continued sucking her breast, but I moved my hand to where hers had been, replacing it and testing how it would feel if it were me touching her.

I felt Sienna tense up again, but I also noticed she was wet, which was a good sign. And it wasn't from the lake water, but a viscous liquid that was lubricating her.

She leaned forward, clinging to me and resting her face on my shoulder.

"I'm scared, Rico."

"Do you want me to stop?"

"No, I don't want you to. I'm enjoying it. That's my fear."

"Fear? No, darling. You *have* to enjoy it. It's your right. You deserve it." Saying this, I replaced one finger with two, touching her with a bit more intensity. I heard her moan softly and felt her teeth on my shoulder, biting me.

"Sorry! I didn't..." She pulled her face away, and I resumed with force, which made her moan louder.

"Bite. Scratch. Do whatever you want with me, Sienna. I'm yours."

I moved my mouth to her neck, using my tongue to kiss her, tasting her skin, while whispering her name like a prayer, moving up to kiss her ear and bite her lobe.

"Try to relax, *Scarlatta*. You're safe with me."

"I know... Oh!" She let out a squeak when I went deeper.

I continued touching her that way until she let out a louder moan, which was almost a lament, a whimper. Her shivers began to increase, and I felt she was reaching orgasm.

She fell apart in my arms, clinging to me, and then lay completely still. I waited for a while, whispering in her ear that everything was okay, and started walking, taking her out of the lake and into the bedroom. I walked slowly, carrying her like a child, giving her the moment she needed.

We were wet, but I didn't care; I just laid her down on the bed and joined her, like we had done the other day, and I realized she was crying.

I raised one hand to dry her face, using the knuckle of my finger.

"Did I hurt you?"

First she swallowed and then shook her head in denial.

"No, you freed me."

I didn't expect to be hit by those words so strongly. I never expected to be anyone's hero. I was the least likely for that, but it was the greatest gift I could receive.

"Then let's take it slow... one step at a time, okay?" I wanted more than anything to be inside her. Even touching her face was painful, but I could wait because I knew it would be worth it.

Everything with her would be worth it.

# CHAPTER TWENTY-TWO

## Enrico

Every time things between Sienna and me took a step forward, it became harder and harder to leave her. Driving home was always a torment, because all I wanted was to take her with me. And it became even more complicated the night I had to leave her after our intimate moment, because my family needed me. My sister's mother was in the hospital, undergoing a kidney transplant, and things were too hectic with Dominic and Alessio having traveled for a mission that could spark an unprecedented war at any moment.

Despite this, I needed to attend to some of Sienna's needs. With all this family chaos, I had to stay away for a couple of days, although we communicated every day. However, it became unfeasible to continue without seeing her, not only because I missed her in a painful way, but because the girl needed supplies.

That time, I had to buy tampons.

I clearly wasn't the right person for this, but it was inevitable, since I was keeping a woman isolated from everything and everyone, with no permission to go out.

I wanted to believe, every time Sienna seemed anxious for me to show up, calling and asking if I would be long, that she missed me. Not as the only person who could provide for her, but as someone she enjoyed the company of, even if she was surrounded by people.

It was pathetic to think I was waiting for crumbs.

And it was those crumbs I wanted to fetch again, even though it had to be a visit almost like a doctor's, because I had things to do that day.

I heard some sounds in the house, but I guessed they were the staff catching up on their routine. I even heard voices coming from the room where Deanna had gone back to sleep since returning to our father's house, to take care of our mother and be protected by us while Dominic traveled with Alessio. I also imagined it could be the girls cleaning and arranging something, because I could swear my sister was at the hospital with Cássia.

If only I had known...

I took my car, after talking to Sienna on the phone for the third time that day, and headed to the cabin, knowing I would have to stop halfway to buy what she needed.

I felt a bit distracted, thinking about a million things at once, especially everything that could happen as a result of the decision that made my brother and my brother-in-law take under their power a nineteen-year-old girl, who had lived her entire life, practically, in a convent, who was very innocent, but was the daughter of a traitor.

I stopped at a store on the way, bought the damned tampons, and went back to the car, continuing to drive.

I only arrived at the cabin, at the spot where I always parked, and entered the house.

Sienna came down the stairs with Lestat in her arms, and I had to take a deep breath, that way I always did when I saw her. Even more so when I found her after what I thought was a considerable amount of time without seeing her.

"Thank you for coming. I hate making you go all this way for something silly. I should have asked before, but I guess I lost track of time..." she said as she approached, placing the cat on the floor.

"I could have calculated it too."

She smiled.

"As if men had much of an understanding of a woman's menstrual cycle." I didn't respond. I knew how it worked, but it was indeed a bit more complicated. We were silent for a few moments, but Sienna soon spoke again. "You're not staying, are you?"

There it was. The feeling I wanted to believe. The one that could easily deceive me. The vulnerable, almost pleading eyes.

She *wanted* me to stay.

"No, *Scarlatta*. I can't." I wanted to say that it broke my heart to have to leave her; that I was eager to spend a few more days there, in our solitary world, just ours. I wanted many things, but I stayed silent, looking at her like the defeated man I was.

An outlaw. Consumed by violence. Owner of hands that had often been stained with blood. How was it possible to love a woman so much? How was it possible for such a pure feeling to live within a tangled mess of chaos and darkness?

Sienna shook her head and her eyes, looking more melancholic than I imagined she would be. I moved closer, positioning myself in front of her and placing one hand on her chin, lifting it so she would look me in the eyes.

"I won't be long. I'm finding out some things..."

The night before, my informant had managed to find out that Fredericco Bonia was a frequent visitor at Dominic's club. This could ensure a good spot for me to find him. It was just a matter of having the right opportunity.

"The concept of being long is different for us, Rico. You have your life, your things. I have... my loneliness."

I had endured different kinds of pain. I had been wounded, cut, shot, bled, nearly perished more than once. Nothing compared to the feeling of hearing her speak like that.

Nothing prepared me for Sienna's outbursts, which were like true daggers sinking into my chest, especially because she wasn't someone who gave in to such confessions. Her suffering was silent, and she held her mask of indifference very well.

Her opening up to me was something I should see as positive. Every time she chose me to be her refuge made our bond tighter. Still, it was hard to ignore how much this affected me in a way that almost forced me to make hasty decisions.

Like taking her away from there and showing her to the world. But I couldn't even dream of making this mistake before proving her innocence.

"Don't look at me like that," she said with a melancholic smile on her face. "It's okay. It's the best version of my life in a long time. Thanks to you."

"You've protected yourself all this time. And you've been making an effort lately. You're a survivor."

"I am. No doubt, I am."

With Sienna's affirmation, with her gaze a bit more determined, I was dying to kiss her. But if I started, I wouldn't be able to stop. The next time I did that, when I could have her for myself, when I could touch her, it would be to go all the way. To convince her she could feel even more pleasure than the first time she reached orgasm.

I placed my hand on her face, looking at her with reverence, and had to say goodbye. I couldn't stay any longer.

I went back to the car, ready to leave, but started to feel a strange movement. I knew I wasn't alone.

But... how?

I moved as far away from the cabin as possible, intending to protect Sienna, although it was futile, as it should be too late. Someone knew our secret—something I had always feared.

I reached for my holster, pulling out my gun as discreetly as possible, taking every precaution so that whoever had followed us and seen that Sienna was alive would not survive to tell the tale.

With calculated movements, I aimed the gun at the person while realizing that the intruder from the car was actually my sister.

"Deanna? *Cazzo Minchia!*" I swore, sure I could have killed her if I hadn't been so careful. "What the hell are you doing here?"

She tried to explain and assured me that her presence there had nothing to do with Dominic. I could see her pajamas and imagine it was an impulsive decision to follow me.

I knew it was wrong for us to be in the middle of the road, stopped and arguing, but my desperation was so strong that I couldn't think of anything else; which was a mistake that could cost us dearly.

We were already without security because that was how I preferred to go on my clandestine visits to that cabin. It was one thing for me to be there unprotected, another for Deanna. My sister was in danger, sent to Los Angeles to be cared for by us.

At that moment, however, all that mattered was Sienna. Exactly for that reason, my guilt when we were caught; when Deanna was pulled from the car, was pure guilt.

I jumped out, still armed, distancing myself and positioning my back to the shoulder, taking advantage of the barrier behind me that would prevent anyone from trying to attack me that way.

"Drop the gun or she dies!" a man said authoritatively, with my sister unconscious in his arms.

They were clearly Cosa Nostra soldiers, especially since the faces of one or two of them were not unfamiliar to me at all. This wasn't a common robbery; it wasn't an act of violence without purpose. Deanna was the target.

"Obey!" the same guy shouted, and I hesitated. If I did that, if I disarmed myself, I couldn't protect Deanna. "Don't test me, Preterotti."

"You're not going to kill her. You know she's too valuable. You know who she's married to," I bluffed.

"Even if she's not killed, there's a lot we can do with her." The bastard started running his hand over my sister's body, which made me grunt and shoot him, losing my head. It was an opportunity, because my aim was very precise.

Even though I hit him, straight in the head, taking advantage of the fact that Deanna was very small and the man who attacked her was quite tall, I knew I couldn't do much more than that.

The man fell backward, a hole in his forehead, and Deanna fell with him, collapsing on top of him. At the same time, I was surrounded even more, taking a punch. I reacted immediately because no one was going to take my sister without me fighting to protect her.

But I was just one. No matter how well-trained, no matter how careful, it was impossible to win.

I swore I would be killed, so that Deanna would be kidnapped, and all I could think about was that Dominic would eventually find his wife.

I knew the reason she was being attacked. Why they wanted to kidnap her. Dominic and Alessio had kidnapped Luna Cipriano. The girl was in their power, and her father wanted her back. Kidnapping my sister was a smart move. They would want to trade her for the other girl or use her for some kind of blackmail with my brother-in-law. Dominic would turn the world upside down to find Deanna, I'd bet all my money on that.

And who would take care of Sienna?

It was her that was on my mind when I was knocked out and when I was forced to surrender and accept my fate.

# CHAPTER TWENTY-THREE

## Enrico

What woke me was the pain.
It wasn't like I could ignore it. Not when I could feel a sharp blade cutting into my chest, tracing a line from one point to another. Not deep enough for me to bleed to death and end their game, but not so superficial that it merely tickled.

I opened my eyes abruptly, letting out a grunt, unable to give myself even a few moments of confusion. The sight of my own blood dripping down my skin was evidence enough that I was in deep trouble.

There was something cylindrical, hard, and cold behind me. A metal bar, judging by the texture and the way my arms were bound behind it, behind my body. Lying on the floor, shirtless, with my hair loose and falling into my face, obstructing my view of my surroundings.

"Awake, Sleeping Beauty?" I slowly lifted my eyes and saw one of the men who had surrounded us on the road. I wanted to look around for Deanna, but for the moment, I needed to focus on the guy. "It wasn't supposed to be like this, you know? We were paid to grab the woman, treat her right, and return her unharmed. But the game changed, didn't it? Now we have not only the queen of the New York mafia with us but also the heir of Los Angeles. So, we don't need to deliver the woman untouched because her little brother is worth as much or more."

"Touch my sister and I'll stomp on you like you're a bug."

The bastard laughed. Taking advantage of his dark amusement, I glanced sideways and saw Deanna lying on the bed, her wrists and ankles bound, with a gag in her mouth. She was still unconscious, wearing the same pajamas she had on when she broke into my car. There were stains of dirt on it, but I looked for any that might look like blood and didn't find any. Thankfully.

"I don't think you're in a position to do that, Shadow Knight."

"I don't need ideal conditions. I just need an *opportunity*."

"You won't get one. You're not dealing with amateurs."

I rarely smiled. But at that moment, one corner of my lips curved up. I didn't expect it to have such a powerful effect because the man tensed up.

Maybe he knew my reputation. Maybe he knew *who* I really was.

I didn't say anything, but my expression, apparently, was enough for retaliation. A liquid was poured directly onto my wound, burning like hell. Still, I kept my eyes fixed on the man. I felt my teeth clenching, my jaw tightening, and I closed my hands into fists, digging my short nails into my palm.

As a provocation, I moved my head so that my eyes were unobstructed and my hair was out of the way.

I took punches, received more cuts, and a piece of hot metal was used to strike me.

When they finally left me alone, I was able to breathe a little and think.

I looked again at Deanna, and she was still unconscious, which provided moments of silence. I closed my eyes, beginning to concentrate, searching for a solution.

There were five men on the road. I had killed one of them. Straining my ears, I tried to hear something, but no sound leaked through, making me believe that the walls were thick.

I needed to know how many there were. I needed to figure out a lot of things before making my decisions.

The second time they came in to check on Deanna, three of them came. I pretended to be asleep to try to learn something. It might seem like a show of weakness to them, but it was worth it to me.

"This wasn't supposed to happen. They shouldn't have brought Enrico Preterotti. They know I can't stay," one of them said.

"The son of a bitch killed Bacco. What could we do? You know he's the devil incarnate. He would definitely find a way to warn Ungaretti, and we'd be screwed."

"What are we going to do with him?" asked the third.

"His father is fucking powerful. The guy is the firstborn, and the other one is useless. Massimo will sell his soul to get the heir back. And the daughter too, of course. We have gold in our hands."

"That might be true, but I can't stay here. It was supposed to be just the girl. We don't have more people. Lazaro had to leave. I have to go handle another job. How are we going to manage?"

"We'll find a way."

That was all I heard after they closed the door.

I looked once more at Deanna and saw her stir. Good sign, one less worry.

I was going to get her out of there. I had enough skills to know I wouldn't be locked up for long. If I were alone, everything would be much easier, but Deanna's safety came first.

The problem was thinking about Sienna. At least my sister already knew she was with me. Although she clearly disapproved of my choice to protect someone everyone considered a traitor, she understood that Deanna was decent enough not to leave another woman helpless.

If I failed, it would have to be Deanna taking care of Sienna.

When my sister woke up, that was my first concern. I needed to ask her to intercede, to show compassion, and to give Sienna a chance. The moment she agreed to that, I felt more confident that I could go to extremes to save her.

The best part was that Deanna wasn't a damsel in distress. She wasn't fragile or foolish. Like Sienna, she was a survivor.

With that in mind, I was able to come up with a plan.

Even when other pains came, even when more of my blood was shed, I remained firm. I heard my sister screaming beside me, seeing me being tortured with a shock weapon, over the wound already inflicted, and having my skin marked to the point of smelling like burned flesh, but I stayed impassive.

Consciousness threatened to abandon me twice when I reached the edge of what was bearable, but still, my determination to show them that I didn't fear them was stronger.

The problem was that I felt once again overtaken by a darkness that Sienna had been soothing recently. The monster I always felt inside me began to threaten to come to the surface again, so much so that when the first opportunity arose, I went after the kidnapper and killed him without mercy.

I would do the same with all of them, but I chose to alert Dominic about our location. I preferred to delay the entry of the others into the room where Deanna and I were, because my brother-in-law would arrive with reinforcements. He would come to help me get her out of there. With a single weapon, we wouldn't get far, especially without a car and with me injured.

It was a gamble. But Deanna would survive, and she had promised to take care of Sienna. That was what mattered.

# CHAPTER TWENTY-FOUR

## Sienna

I stayed by the window for a long time, staring into nothingness after Enrico's visit, which was so brief it felt almost like a breath.

I should be used to solitude. Considering everything I've been through and what I might still face, working in that place, after being literally auctioned off, that peace was welcome. I knew things would be easier if I hadn't fallen in love.

Or fallen in love again. Twice, Enrico had been the messenger of illusions in my mind. He was both the demon and the angel that lived in my head, provoking me towards right and wrong.

I should have fought and resisted, especially since things were starting to get too physical. But I couldn't get those moments we spent by the lake out of my head. Not in a bad way, actually, as I always imagined would happen when I decided to let myself be seduced.

It was intoxicating. I still knew almost nothing about sex and pleasure, but I could understand something I'd never been able to before: why people become so addicted, why they surrender so completely.

Since the moment he left, through the next day, for hours and hours, I stayed with my elbow resting on the windowsill, holding my head, with Lestat by my side, like a maiden waiting for her lover to return from war.

A maiden who had technology on her side but hadn't received any calls or messages in almost twenty-four hours. It wasn't typical of Enrico, but I knew things between the Ungaretti and Preterotti families weren't going well. I had to be patient.

It was almost five in the afternoon the next day when I sighed and went up to my room to change. I put on my leggings, a top, and tied up my hair, which had grown even longer since I arrived at the cabin. I grabbed the mat, a water bottle, and other supplies, and went outside. It would soon be evening, and I liked to watch the sunset over the lake, especially while working out. Even though it had been a short time since we started the training, I could already feel, the differences in stamina, conditioning, and even strength.

I started with stretching and a bit of meditation. Then I would move on to strength and aerobic training. It was much better to do all of that with Enrico present, with company, but I had to manage.

While I was still sitting cross-legged, with my eyes closed and breathing rhythmically to the sound of relaxing music, I was startled by a tightness in my chest, as if something was wrong.

I put my hand over my heart, feeling it race and my breath become uncertain. I even got up, standing and interrupting the meditation. Lestat, as if sensing my unusual agitation, came over, rubbing against my legs, but even that couldn't calm me.

I grabbed my phone, which was nearby, and started trying to call him, only to get the metallic, recorded voice telling me the phone was going to voicemail.

I tried texting, more than once, starting to feel like a crazy, controlling person.

But it had been too long without any news. A deafening silence.

I wanted to try to go back to my activities, but a wave of intense anxiety overwhelmed me. It was as if I felt that Enrico wasn't okay; as if something inside me warned that we would have very unpleasant surprises.

At that moment, I should have started thinking about what would happen if he were seriously injured or worse... Being isolated like I was, how would I survive? Of course, there was the emergency training, the way to call a car to pick me up, and if I wanted to, I could escape. There was money at my disposal, and I wasn't a weak woman anymore. I could defend myself as best as possible.

Even so, leaving my refuge would mean having to return to civilization. And if someone recognized me? If I were caught and cornered?

All of that should have occurred to me immediately, but my concern for Enrico was stronger.

Every hour that passed, every moment without news, drove me into panic. Enrico was undoubtedly one of the most capable men I knew when it came to protecting himself. He had skills that, without a doubt, I could never even dream of, but he was still human. Mortal. Not invincible.

I couldn't say how many hours I spent in agony like that, but it was more than a day. Maybe I could say three if I had been paying attention to the clock.

When I heard the sound of car wheels crunching on gravel, the first thing I did was grab the revolver Enrico left for me, arming myself. With no news for so long, anything could have happened, including the discovery of my hideout. I needed to be prepared; after all, I had been trained for this.

It was raining outside. A storm of thunder, lightning, and rain. An ill omen? I didn't want to think of it that way, but I was scared enough to do so.

I locked Lestat in the bathroom— the only way I could protect him for as long as possible—and took my position behind the couch.

For a few minutes, absolutely nothing happened, which only made me more and more terrified. If it were Enrico, he would have jumped out by now, without a doubt.

Why the delay?

I started moving closer to the window, trying to make as little noise as possible, hoping the sounds of the storm would provide cover. The car remained parked there, with the windows closed, as if it had appeared on its own, having taken a road with no driver at the wheel. As if it were haunted.

I was startled when the sound of the horn blared continuously, almost like an alarm. I had to cover my mouth to stifle a strangled sound that escaped my throat.

Then I covered my ears because the damn noise wouldn't stop. What if it was a way to lure me into a trap? What if someone was trying, somehow, to corner me?

I stood still, thinking I couldn't act rashly, until the driver's window began to open. It wasn't all the way, just a bit. Enough for me to recognize Enrico's somewhat long hair, dirty and oily, covering his face, which seemed to be slumped over the steering wheel, as if he were injured.

Again... it could be a trap. Someone might have put themselves next to him and forced him to come to me, but I suspected he would die before doing that.

So, I ran outside, still with the gun in hand, approaching the car, feeling the rain soaking me from head to toe.

I quickly confirmed he was alone. And injured. Very injured.

I opened the door and pushed him to lean against the seat, and saw him shirtless, with his chest covered in wounds. I put the gun away to check his condition better, trembling and frightened, noticing marks on his arm as if an intravenous line had been placed there. The face I found so stunning was wounded, bruised, and cut, but his chest was the most concerning. I didn't know if it needed stitches. There were burns, all kinds of marks, which I feared would become even more scars than the ones he already had.

"Rico? What happened? Please... talk to me!" I said, though I was visibly desperate, even though I wasn't one to show my emotions.

I had to brush away another stubborn lock of hair that fell over his eyes while watching him open them weakly, vulnerably, in a way I never imagined he could be.

I also had to brush my own eyes, which were soaking wet because of the relentless rain.

"I don't know how I got here, Sienna. But I needed you. I *wanted* you."

"What you *need* is a hospital."

"No!" Enrico growled. He had to take a deep breath to do so, as even speaking was undoubtedly painful. How was it possible that he had driven so many miles in that condition? "You, Sienna. I need you."

I felt his consciousness waver for a moment, which terrified me even more.

"Rico? No, please. You need to help me. I can't get you out of the car alone. It's too heavy for me."

It was almost cruel to ask something of him, but how was I going to get him to bed? At least the room where I slept was on the ground floor, because there would be no chance I could manage to carry a man over six feet tall up the stairs.

Still, he managed to move. It was a slow process, and I could swear he was feeling excruciating pain without complaining. He didn't show on his beautiful, wounded face the suffering I imagined he was enduring.

Enrico was a man of iron. So I needed to be strong for him, too.

The man had protected me from everything and everyone. He had saved me in every possible way.

It was my time to give back.

# CHAPTER TWENTY-FIVE

## Enrico

Fever.

I knew I had a fever.

At the same time that chills spread through my body and made my teeth chatter, I was burning up, as if I were inside a bonfire. My forehead was soaked, and sometimes a fleeting sense of relief would overcome me when a damp cloth was pressed against it. Just as when Sienna made me take medicine, making every effort to help me rise from the bed just enough to prevent the water from overflowing and soaking me entirely.

Her voice... That was what kept me tethered to reality.

Her scent.

Her touch.

It was for her that I fought.

Not that I intended to give up. But if it weren't for Sienna, I certainly wouldn't be entering the ring against death so determinedly. The certainty that I still had the mission to protect her and keep her safe in the midst of this cruel and intimidating world we lived in was the crutch I used to walk down the path that would return me to reality.

Just as the need to keep my sister safe had made me endure every minute of the torture I was subjected to.

Days seemed lost between the threshold of light and darkness. The latter had been my long-time friend. Since I was initiated, I wandered through it, in a straight line, always with firm steps. When Sienna arrived, and again when I met her again, I felt intoxicated, stumbling, almost swaying towards the beams of light that extended around me, trying to capture me.

At that moment, the lights were my path to life. And I saw Sienna's face, along with her outstretched hands, at the end of each of them.

She read to me for hours and hours. Sitting beside me, attentive and worried—by what I could sense in her tone of voice. She prayed too, though I had the impression she wasn't a devout woman.

I just needed to move so that she would jump up and come to me. To place her delicate hands on my face and whisper that everything would be okay, that she was there for me.

Strong. My survivor.

My woman.

It didn't matter what was happening around us. It didn't matter that the world was against us, ready to swallow us whole. She was *mine*. I would fight for her the same way I was fighting for my life. And one thing was the consequence of the other.

"Scarlatta..." I whispered, with my eyes closed, not even knowing if she was in the room. But Sienna was tireless. I had the impression she hadn't slept properly in days.

It took only seconds for me to feel her by my side. Her hand closed around mine, and the sensation was as always: safety, home, relief. Any pain was bearable with her around. That's why I couldn't stay in the damned hospital my father tried to take me to.

I stayed only a few hours, just enough to find out if Deanna would recover, and then I left. I disappeared, stealing a car from the parking lot and heading to the cabin, sure that Sienna would be my cure.

"I'm here, Rico. What do you need?"

"You need to rest," I said with my few remaining bits of strength, my voice coming out as a whisper, hoarse and broken.

I heard her give a soft laugh.

"I'm not tired."

"Impossible."

"Not at all. I had a good lesson in endurance. If it were before, I would have been lying on the ground exhausted. Now I'm steady."

I shifted in bed, slowly opening my eyes. The first thing they saw, after pulling away from the darkness, was Sienna's face.

Of course, she was tired. Pale. With dark circles. Her red hair had been tied up in a bun, with some strands escaping and hanging in her face. She looked at me with eyes full of various emotions, which made me feel even more vulnerable than I did, although I was almost sure I was better compared to when I arrived.

If there was anything more beautiful than her at that moment, I was unaware of it.

"You're strong. You've always been," I said, lifting my hand and touching her face.

Sienna tilted her head to the side, accepting my affection and sighing.

"And you, Enrico? You arrived here nearly dead. I was afraid of losing you." My chest ached with that confession. "What happened?"

"I was k-kidnapped with Deanna."

"Oh, God! How is she?" she asked with visible concern.

"She was... injured when I left her, but recovering." I needed to pause to breathe. "My father, Dominic, and Alessio will take care of her."

"Who kidnapped you?"

"I imagine it was someone acting on Pietro Cipriano's orders. But things are much deeper than that." I felt myself starting to get agitated, so I shifted in bed again, which made Sienna place her hand on my bare chest.

"Don't exert yourself. We can talk later. You're getting better."

"I need to talk now. It's important..." I paused again to catch my breath. I imagined my eyes must have looked glazed, heavy, and with some hint of desperation, but the situation demanded all of it. "Deanna found out. She came here hidden in my car. It was after leaving here that they took us."

Sienna took a step back, visibly frightened.

"Do you think she'll tell anyone? Dominic?"

"I don't know. I plan to talk to her as soon as I can."

"And what if she has already told them? If they already know?"

"Then they would have come after us."

I didn't want to scare her, but it was too late. As I paced back and forth, twisting the strand of hair that fell into my eyes around a finger, breathing uncertainly, all I wanted was to take back my words and pretend nothing was happening, but she needed to know.

Even though I believed I was out of danger, leaving her in the dark could cost her life. On alert, Sienna might react if I were to falter in any way. Or if someone showed up while I was still convalescent, she would have means to defend herself.

"I've discovered some things," I revealed, which made her stop and look at me. "I hadn't said anything yet, but I think we're about to make progress in the investigation. The bastard who hurt you is a regular at Dominic's club. I think I might find a way to corner him."

"And what do you think we can gain from that?"

"Maybe get him to talk. If he reveals what he knows, it might clear you."

"It would be the word of a traitor, Rico."

"It doesn't matter. Either way, I want him in my hands." And speaking of hands, I took hers in mine, intertwining our fingers. I didn't have the strength for much, but it felt almost necessary. "I'm going to make him pay, Sienna. It's a debt he'll regret ever incurring."

"We will. I can't let you handle this alone without getting my hands on one of the men who destroyed me. I want to be part of everything. You're training me for this, aren't you?"

Yes, I was. I could use the excuse that it was to help her defend herself, but it wasn't just that. I really wanted Sienna to be strong and resilient enough to seek revenge, if she wished.

I would never underestimate her.

"I am, Scarlatta. When the time comes, you can be by my side, if you want."

"I do."

Then so it would be.

# CHAPTER TWENTY-SIX

## Sienna

Enrico's recovery process was much quicker than I initially thought. I had the impression that this was mainly due to his determination to get better, for my sake.

Every day he got out of bed, ready for his walks to strengthen his limbs, he made it clear to me that he couldn't weaken because he needed to protect me.

I should have felt bad about this, not only because I knew he was exerting himself more than necessary to speed up the process but also because I wanted him to trust that I could defend myself. Despite this, I knew I wasn't prepared to fight the Cosa Nostra on my own, with its trained men, and as fragile as it might sound, I loved that he took care of me that way.

His wounds were healing, and his body was getting stronger. Within a week, he was going up and down the stairs, even though it drove me crazy. In nine days, I caught him doing pull-ups outside, on a structure he had set up for me.

"Enrico! For God's sake! What are you doing? Are you trying to kill yourself?" I raised my voice, making it rise an octave unintentionally.

But he was certainly going to drive me crazy. He was far from the man who had arrived almost dead days earlier.

He was a bit more breathless than before, but his arms lifted his body weight with ease, and the only thing that reminded me of his dark moments were the new scars. Especially the one on his chest, which I had to search on YouTube for the right way to care for, as the stitches done at the hospital had come apart, and I had to stitch it up again.

I don't even know how I managed to keep my hands steady for that.

Without his shirt, he dropped the bar, stepping on the ground barefoot and wiping one hand on the other. Still silent, he let his hair down, which was barely sweaty, and tied it up again in that samurai bun that was a delight.

I wanted to say something more, but my words got stuck in my throat, while my stomach churned looking at him.

Those narrow eyes looked at me with an insane amount of intensity; something that always emanated from him. I wasn't lying when I said I was terrified of losing him. Seeing him injured and showing a vulnerability I had never seen before confirmed a feeling that was no longer a doubt but still scared me to admit.

But the fact that he was so attractive drained all my discernment and made me believe that surrendering would be a smarter choice than fighting against it.

Even if this surrender clashed with some of my deepest convictions.

Enrico took a step toward me, as serious as ever.

"I'm fine. Staying out of shape is not an option"—his response was almost rude, but I knew it wasn't directed at me. It was his way of showing me it wasn't a choice.

Removing the glove he had been wearing and setting it aside, I watched him walk closer and closer to me, completely uninjured, not even limping. It was admirable.

"You're feeling much better, I imagine," I said, with a hint of sarcasm in my voice. Even a bit of mockery.

"One hundred percent."

That was very dangerous.

Very much so.

He was about to pass me, probably to get something in the kitchen, but I positioned myself in his way. It was a very instinctive, almost automatic move, and I tilted my head to look at him better.

I parted my lips, letting out a long sigh, wishing more than ever to be kissed. Wishing that Enrico would pull me to him and stop treating me like the fragile crystal I knew he considered me to be.

His precious, broken porcelain doll. I still didn't know how far I could go, but I needed to feel more than he had given me that day, which seemed like it had happened an eternity ago.

When I took another step forward, we were so close that I could feel the heat emanating from his skin. I could feel the vibration coming from his body toward mine.

I could touch him. I could indicate that I wanted him to touch me too. I could guide one of his hands to my breast, slipping it under my shirt, which should be about two sizes larger than mine. I could encourage him to grab my hips and press his lips against mine.

I didn't do any of that, though. But my gaze said everything I couldn't voice.

"What are you doing, Sienna? Are you trying to tempt me?" Enrico got the message.

"If you want me, you'll have to take what you want." He was about to say something, but I silenced him by placing a finger on his mouth. "No hesitations. Show me what you would do to me if I weren't a broken woman."

Enrico let out a bitter laugh.

"You probably wouldn't want to know"—his voice came out so hoarse it was almost guttural.

"I want to. Because you're the only one who can make me feel normal, Rico. You gave me pleasure, something I never imagined would happen. But I want more."

"I can give you more..." He lowered his eyes directly to my mouth. The depth of his tone left me almost dizzy.

"I want it. But I really want it. I won't fall apart because you'll be there to piece me back together. Just grant my request. Don't make me beg."

"I would never do that."

"Then... what are you waiting for?"

Enrico hesitated for two seconds. Maybe a bit longer, but it was a very brief time, because all I felt next was his hand reaching up to my neck. I was pulled in, and as my body moved closer to his, his arm hooked around my waist.

Almost at the same moment his mouth sought mine, I was lifted off the ground by that possessive arm, and he carried me like that to the counter, where he set me down.

With his hands free, Enrico grabbed a lock of my hair, pulling it back, making me arch my head. It was a submissive position, but I didn't feel scared by it. Not in the least. I wanted *more*.

"I told you not to treat me like porcelain, but you didn't have to go overboard being..." I said when he pulled away a bit, but before I could finish, he attacked my lips again, demanding entry and using his tongue to play with mine.

His other hand slid to my breast, beneath the hem of my shirt, and his thumb rubbed against the lace of my bra, creating friction that made me shiver.

The kiss continued, and I didn't want it to end. I didn't want Enrico to pull away from me, but I changed my mind almost immediately when I felt him focusing on my neck, using his tongue and even his teeth to seduce me.

"I want to taste all of you. I'm going to suck you, Sienna, until you pass out in my arms. You don't know how much I've wanted this and for how long."

"I don't know the sensation, Enrico. Show me..."

I didn't need to ask twice. Eagerly, he removed my shirt, throwing it to the floor, and did the same with my bra. His mouth sought my nipple, and he sucked with such fervor that it almost seemed like anger. I let out a moan, which for a moment I swore was out of fear, but the way my core throbbed, it was something else entirely.

Enrico couldn't keep his mouth and hands in one place. He seemed like a ravenous madman, kissing me all over, as if he wanted to taste every inch of my skin, leaving nothing untouched.

The sounds he made, the way his fingers gripped me, how he kept pulling my hair... He was fulfilling my request.

He grabbed my clothes again, removing my shorts and panties, doing so almost with hatred, as if the clothing were a barrier between him and what he wanted.

"I'm going to touch you the way you touched yourself. Can I?" It was sweet of him to ask, but I could barely find the composure to answer, so I just nodded.

He seemed satisfied with my response because he used his middle finger to penetrate me. No matter how desperate he was, he buried it deep but slowly, respecting my limits and checking my reactions.

For a second, my body tensed, but I was glad Enrico didn't give up. That he continued.

I dug my nails into his shoulders, wanting to pull him closer, just to feel his body. His arm muscles were also the target of my touch, and I didn't try to hide how much I wanted to feel them.

Enrico was a rock. No matter how strong I felt compared to before, I was still small and feminine next to him.

His thumb massaged my clitoris while two of his fingers thrust forcefully, and his mouth sucked on my nipple. The confusion of sensations was like a tornado, and I struggled to arch my body, but I felt weak, languid. Which was not a problem for Enrico, because he put one arm under my hips and lifted me off the counter, with his free arm, raising me a bit higher, which made the sensations even more unbearable. In the best way.

It was such delicious torture that I kept wondering when things would start to go wrong, as I had never found pleasure like this before.

But also... it was the first time I was giving my body to someone willingly, which made my reactions more than understandable.

Not only that. I loved Enrico.

It was something that only started to make sense in my head after I almost lost him.

It didn't matter how I realized it; the truth was I couldn't imagine my life without him anymore. Even if I returned to reality, if I left that hideaway, without Enrico, I would be lost. Confused. I would be half of myself again.

Still holding me in his arms, he carried me off the counter and towards the stairs. No matter how much I trusted him, no matter how much I knew who I was with, the thought of being in a bed, even if it was in a completely different room from where I was assaulted, began to scare me.

Everything would probably be okay because I would look into Enrico's eyes and know whose arms I was in. Even so, I didn't want anything to ruin the moment.

"Don't take me to the bed, please."

Enrico stopped immediately, in the middle of the stairs, and I quickly regretted saying anything. I feared he would give up completely on what we were doing, but he didn't even respond, just laid me down on one of the steps, higher up, and settled below me.

He removed his sweatpants, folded them, and placed them on one of the steps.

"Kneel here."

I had no idea what his intentions might be, but I obeyed. Enrico placed his hand on my back, forcing me to lean forward, to be on all fours. It was a position of submission, but he wouldn't be on top of me. He wouldn't press me into a bed. I understood what his strategy was.

But I didn't expect what his ideas would be.

"I want you to massage your clitoris while I suck you. Can you do that, *Scarlatta*?"

"I-I can..." I even stammered, but I couldn't move until Enrico positioned himself, spreading my legs and placing himself between them, lying on the stairs, on his back, able to dive into me however he wanted.

The moment he began to suck me, I did what he asked, using my fingers to touch myself.

I had control over one part, while he had control over another. It started out delicious but quickly became almost violent because I couldn't keep my movements just gentle. I couldn't stay silent as he sucked me as if his survival depended on it.

"Can you just stay on your knees?" he asked, interrupting the oral sex for a few moments.

"I think so."

"Try. And use your other hand to touch your nipples. One and then the other."

I couldn't endure it. Still, I wanted to try.

The scream I let out when I massaged my nipple with almost painful force echoed through the house. If it had been Enrico doing it, it would have been even better, but I understood all the reasons he wanted it to be me.

Enrico had taught me to find pleasure on my own. Then he decided to teach me that it was possible for us to share that "responsibility." He was saving me again.

I was like a castaway rescued at sea. He was my lifeboat.

I orgasmed even more than the first time, and I barely managed to recover when I was picked up and carried outside the house, with my legs wrapped around his waist, taken to the bar where Enrico had worked out earlier.

"Raise your arms and hold on. I'm going to fuck you standing up. Will you be comfortable with that?"

"I-I don't know... I didn't know that..."

"That it was possible? Yes, it's possible."

Enrico didn't say anything about condoms because he knew I was on birth control. Since the first time I was raped by my brother, I've never stopped taking it. Even though Bruno wasn't my blood relative and had been adopted, having a child by him would be a death sentence for me.

So, I held on exactly as he instructed, and the first thing Enrico did was bring his mouth to my nipples, one at a time.

"I was envious of your fingers, *Scarlatta*," he whispered like velvet, and I gasped.

Then, while still sucking on those sensitive points, he positioned himself inside me.

He was large, demanding space, and I braced myself for pain, as always happened, but I was so wet that Enrico's cock slid in effortlessly, finding the deepest point inside me.

Holding me by the thighs and firmly, Enrico moved me, thrusting in and out, out and in with force. The moment he thrust, the pleasure was so intense that I screamed loudly and almost let go of the bar. Not that he would let me fall, but in that position, he had more freedom to make things more voracious.

"*Dio Santo*, Sienna. It's painful how much I desire you. How much I've always wanted to be inside you," Enrico said in a growl, bringing his mouth to my neck, kissing me as he truly fucked me, just as he had said he would.

The movements grew more intense, and I felt the friction of flesh against flesh; I heard the sounds of our bodies colliding as I threw my head back, closed my eyes, and surrendered.

Even though I knew Enrico had an insane desire for me, that all of this was demanding immense control from him, he didn't give in quickly. He enjoyed each thrust as much as I was enjoying. He took from me as much as I was taking from him.

In the end, it was hard to know who saved whom.

When I came again, followed by a few more thrusts from him, I felt as if those moments had created a barrier between who we were before and after them.

We were more connected than ever.

# CHAPTER TWENTY-SEVEN

## Enrico

Two weeks after the kidnapping, I returned home. There were no questions, no criticism for disappearing, and these should have been the biggest indications that people already knew exactly who I was.

I worried about what Deanna might have said about what she discovered, but up to that point, she had kept it a secret. Her condition for staying silent was meeting Sienna, which needed to happen quickly, since my sister would be returning to New York after Pietro Cipriano was killed by Dominic.

As far as everyone knew, the threat had been contained.

I still had my doubts after Sienna's report. My impression was that there were many more secrets to be revealed. And that most of them would put us in dangerous situations.

The times ahead had much potential to be dark. Or even *darker*.

My concern at that moment was how I would get Deanna out of my father's house and take her to the cabin, alone, with absolutely no security following us. Dominic seemed like a vulture circling his wife after she had been caught, and even with me, it wouldn't be easy to get her out of the excessive protection he had put in place.

The way I managed it was in the middle of the night. Just as I had entered the car, hidden, it had to be that way. Dominic needed to have a meeting with Luna's brothers about the return of the girl – which was a complicated word, but the correct concept – and he wouldn't be sleeping next to his wife.

Deanna cooperated with the plan, and at the right time, she was in my car, lying in the back seat, covered with a blanket, escaping as if she were a fugitive.

Was it dangerous? Yes. We had already experienced the worst that could happen when caught off guard, and I didn't want to put my sister at risk again. But if her condition was to meet Sienna and talk to her before deciding whether to come clean to Dominic, there was no choice.

"We're free," I said to her as I drove, and Deanna shifted, moving to the front seat, adjusting herself and buckling up.

"Good. You know Dominic will kill you if he finds out, right?"

"It wouldn't be good for you either."

"Oh, don't underestimate me, *fratello*. I'd say you kidnapped me." Of course, she was joking, and I knew that mainly because of her mischievous smile. But knowing Deanna, anything could have a hint of truth. "But tell me... what do I need to know about your Sienna before meeting her?"

"That she's innocent," I said with such conviction that it seemed to surprise her.

Deanna sighed.

"You love her." It wasn't a question.

"Desperately. But I'm not blind. I'm not basing my judgment on my feelings."

She nodded, and we continued driving. I had made it clear that I didn't care what happened. If I needed to turn our lives into a war; if I needed to die and kill, that's what I would do, because it would be worth it.

A large part of the trip was in silence because my sister and I didn't exactly have a topic of conversation, and I knew we were both tense.

It was past three in the morning when we arrived at the cabin, and I hoped Sienna had managed to stay awake.

When I opened the door, she was actually pacing back and forth, nervous, being followed by the cat, who quickly went to inspect who the woman beside me was, suspicious and territorial.

I had been living with Sienna for some time. To be honest, I had known her for many years and had the right and privilege to understand her a little better; to see nuances in the girl and the woman that others might not be able to see.

I knew that behind her cold and indifferent facade was a warm woman who had dedicated herself immensely to taking care of me when I needed it; someone frightened, vulnerable, but who fought every day to strengthen herself and overcome her terrors.

Gradually, that more human side of Sienna started to stand out. Each day we met, especially during the time I spent by her side recovering, I watched that kind and sweet personality take control. At that moment, however, upon meeting the new queen of the Cosa Nostra in New York, Sienna tensed, lifted her head, proud, wearing her mask and her armor.

"You must be Sienna..." Deanna said, crossing her arms. "You don't look like a traitor. I came from afar and had my sleep interrupted just to meet you. I hope you do a good job proving to me that the entire Cosa Nostra is wrong about you." My sister's tone was intimidating. Not that I ever doubted it, but she was fitting into her hierarchical position very well. The aura of power that surrounded Dominic was gradually molding into her personality, and I knew she would serve our organization with great fierceness and determination.

"I am. I have a story to tell you, which I hope will be enough."

I saw her swallow hard, visibly scared of what was about to happen. She would once again have to recount something that tormented her, and on top of that, to a complete stranger.

"Sienna..." I said in a reproachful tone, hoping she would be cautious.

"I'm fine, Enrico. You trust Deanna, don't you?"

I cast a glance at my sister, realizing she was also watching me.

"I trust her. The question is whether *she* trusts me."

It stopped being about Sienna for a few moments and began to turn into a conversation between two siblings who had their hesitations about each other.

It became a test of brotherhood.

Deanna hesitated, and I felt my chest tighten.

"I trust her. Literally my life."

I took a deep breath, my heart racing. It was hard to surrender to emotions like that, but I had some attachment to Deanna. Maybe a greater attachment than would be prudent, because despite being siblings, our bond wasn't that deep.

Still, we had faced real danger together, and I would do anything to protect her.

"I'm excited to hear your story, Sienna..." Deanna threw herself on the couch, petting Lestat, who was already there, settled in.

Sienna smiled darkly, looking at her.

"I imagine you won't be excited after hearing it, or I hope you won't be. But here we go..."

"I'm all ears," my sister replied, and I decided to step away, not only because I wasn't ready to hear the full tragedy of Sienna's life again, but because I believed this was their moment.

I moved away, staying near the lake, waiting to see what the outcome of the meeting would be. Whether Deanna would stand with us or against us.

# CHAPTER TWENTY-EIGHT

## Sienna

Face to face, two women who didn't know each other but needed to share a huge secret. It was ironic to think that, from that moment on, my life would be in the hands of someone whose name I only knew.

Lies. I knew much more about Deanna Preterotti.

She was the sister of the man I loved, who was giving everything he had to protect me. He trusted her, too.

At the same time, she was the wife of someone I could consider an enemy. A man whose power was unimaginable and who believed I was involved in the attack on his cousin's life, someone he loved.

I was the prey, after all, of very dangerous predators. The traps were within my reach, ready for me to fall into them and get lost.

Looking into Deanna's eyes, I saw much of myself. No doubt we were very different, but she was strong in her own way. We had lived different experiences, yet in the end, we were two women trying to survive in a dark world dominated by men who wanted to control us.

"I'm waiting, Sienna. You should understand that I don't have much time. I still need to get home without being seen, or I'll have to come up with a very good story for my husband before he finds out about you."

"Do you want to know the details? Because they're dirty."

"How dirty?"

"Like when a man got on top of me, taking my virginity in the most painful way possible, without my consent. And then others, later, also raped me, on the same day, enjoying themselves at my expense."

I saw Deanna's mouth drop open in a silent exclamation, surprised, holding her breath.

"I'm sorry," she said.

"People usually feel sorry when someone says they were raped, but I never even had the chance to talk about it, because I had to run away."

"Why did you run away? Couldn't anyone offer you protection?"

I let out a bitter laugh, settling in front of her.

"It doesn't work like that. In the Cosa Nostra, they shoot first and ask questions later. It was easier to see me as the viper sister of the traitor than as a woman who lived years in hiding, raped by that same brother."

"Was it him? He who..."

"Raped me. You can use the word. It doesn't matter what you call it. But yes, it was him. We weren't biological siblings, but that was beside the point. Living with him, under his roof, knowing he wasn't allowing me to marry anyone... that was far worse. And I wanted to get married. To anyone who would take me. None of them would be worse than Bruno."

"I'm really sorry, Sienna. No woman deserves to go through that."

"No, she doesn't. But I survived. I'm here. Today, thanks to your brother, but I don't credit him alone, because I know I did a lot on my own. And I want to do more..."

I told Deanna the little I knew. I spoke about the conversations I'd overheard at my house, about what Enrico had discovered up to that point, and about my need for revenge. Our training was also mentioned, and she listened to me attentively.

I didn't want to have hopes that she would help me, that she would agree to keep such a big secret from Dominic. So when I finished speaking, I looked at her anxiously, fidgeting with my hands.

"He's a member of Dominic's club, right?" I had already said that, but if she needed confirmation, I nodded, curious to know where her thoughts were heading. "We'll have a party in a few days. I don't think Enrico knows about it."

"He didn't tell me anything."

"Well, only members know. Interestingly, it will be a masquerade ball. I can try to find out if that son of a bitch will be there."

"And what would we do?" I began to get excited, in a rather morbid way, even shifting in my seat.

"If you want to get involved, you could go with Enrico. A wig, a mask... maybe they won't recognize you. At least that's what I would do."

She was crazy.

But I liked the idea.

"And if they recognize me? I'll be dead."

"Not if I can help it. What worries me is the kind of things you'll see there. People don't engage in conventional sex. Do you think that might trigger you?"

I hesitated before answering, because I didn't know what my reaction would be in such a situation, especially after having such a liberating experience with Enrico.

"I'll survive. Again."

"I don't doubt it. The bigger problem? Convincing Enrico of that."

"He's training me; it's unlikely he'll veto it."

Deanna broke into a smile followed by a cynical laugh.

"You've been in this world longer than I have, Sienna. It's not possible you don't understand how our men are. If he doesn't lock you up in this house to keep you from putting yourself at risk, I'd be surprised."

"Enrico will respect my wishes..."

At least, that's what I thought.

I swear I thought so.

But that certainty lasted only until we called him back and told him the plan.

I watched Enrico's handsome face turn red, and his eyes widened. His large hands clenched into fists, the joints turning white from the force he was exerting.

"Not a chance! That's not an option. Deanna, stop putting crazy ideas in Sienna's head!" His voice came out in a growl that startled me so much I leaned back, hand on my chest.

"Deanna didn't do anything. I *want* to. I have my own will, if you didn't know..." I asserted with all the calm in the world, resuming my usual stance. I knew I could never win an argument by losing my temper, especially not against Enrico. "I'm going to crash that party one way or another, Enrico. I'd like to count on your help, if possible."

He moved closer to me, standing face to face. Our noses almost touched, especially because he leaned his body, aligning our heights.

"They'll recognize you, Sienna. You'll be in danger, and I won't be able to do anything."

"But I can. Who are the people who could harm Sienna? Dominic and Giovanni. Kiara is thrilled about the party, so the men will be quite occupied, believe me. I have some ideas, too, to keep other people distracted as well. We can come up with a good plan and..."

"Deanna!" Enrico reprimanded his sister, and I could swear he was ready to set the whole house on fire with us inside.

That also made me angry.

"You know what, Enrico?" I raised a finger, touching it to his chest. "You took me out of where I was, brought me to this house, where I'm nothing more than a prisoner. And for what? I was already dead before, but now I have a chance to get revenge on those who wronged me."

"I can take revenge for you," he said through clenched teeth.

"So why did you start training me?"

"Because I want you to know how to defend yourself and not just attack! I want you to be strong, to not be vulnerable, but not to throw yourself into the lion's den."

"I'm not porcelain!"

"Of course you're not, and I've never treated you like that. But any of us could be in danger if we put ourselves in a situation like this. I'm not underestimating you."

"Hey, hey, hey!" Deanna interrupted us, getting up. I quickly noticed that she was holding my cat in her lap.

Lestat wouldn't let anyone hold him like that, except for me, but he was definitely standing still like a statue in the woman's arms.

"I'm taking this cutie outside because you two are having a drama that I don't want to be a part of." We fell silent, watching her, and Deanna headed for the door. When she was almost at the door, she made a hand gesture as if to brush away the air, saying: "Continue, continue..."

Enrico and I remained staring at the door for a while, somewhat dazed, and I began to think that this was the effect she had on people.

It took a few moments before he turned back to me, with a slightly calmer but still tense expression, his jaw clenched:

"Don't put yourself at risk, *Scarlatta*. — It's very hard to stay immune to him when he calls me that nickname."

Even so, I needed to stay firm.

"We can come up with a plan that keeps us safe. It's a masquerade ball, Rico. You'll be nearby, Deanna is on our side. I want to get revenge; it's my right after everything I've been through."

"A lot can go wrong," he whispered, raising his hand and touching my face with the back of his fingers. "I can't lose you. I can't bear to see you hurt."

I closed my eyes, absorbing the caress, sighing.

"It's my right..." I repeated because I would insist on that point. Enrico couldn't deny me.

"We'll talk. If it's a good plan, we'll find a way."

"Yes, we'll find a way..."

No matter how good the plan was, I was going. It would be my moment to turn the tables, and I had been living for that ever since I managed to escape.

The time would come.

# CHAPTER TWENTY-NINE

## Sienna

There I was again with the blonde wig. It was different from the one I wore back when I worked at the club, and I had to admit it suited me much better. The old one was platinum, unrefined; the new one, which Enrico had managed to get, had a beautiful golden hue with darker highlights and a side fringe. It completely hid my red hair, just as the mask disguised my face as best as possible. It was large, golden, covered in jewels and details. It even covered a little below my nose, and I had deliberately chosen a lipstick color that wasn't my usual shade, hoping it would offer me even more protection.

I was a bit slimmer than I had been when I attended Cosa Nostra parties, but the dress I chose was low-cut, accentuated my curves, and had a large slit up one leg. Gloves covered my hands, although it was almost impossible for anyone to recognize me like this, unless fingerprints were analyzed.

Still, every precaution was worth it.

I needed to enter separately from Enrico or I'd attract too much attention. No doubt his brother Dominic and anyone else would be interested in knowing who the Shadow Knight's companion was, as he was never seen with anyone.

To be honest, I would have felt a bit better with him by my side, but I made every effort not to show my insecurities, especially because that would be my undoing. Not just to keep Enrico from cutting me off but also to avoid raising suspicions.

That night I was Scarlett again; a daring and curious girl wanting to get involved with a mobster, to venture into the world of an outlaw.

My focus was singular, though. Fredericco Bonia. Of the bastards who hurt me, he was the only one whose face could be part of my nightmares, except for Bruno.

It wouldn't be hard to find him.

My entry was granted because Deanna had arranged it. I had a VIP invitation, which gave me access to all floors of the club and private rooms if I wished. Of course, I didn't. I had no idea what went on inside, but I imagined it would be a bit too much for me. Especially without Enrico.

I walked through the ballroom, finding it not much different from the club where I danced, except that it had a clientele of well-dressed men drinking whiskies more expensive than the salary of the waiters, and the atmosphere was more refined. There was a girl on stage, dancing nude, clinging to a pole, and she was beautiful. Also an excellent dancer. Because of her toned legs, I had no doubt she was a professional ballerina making good money to be there.

There were other naked girls sitting on men's laps, others walking around in just lingerie, holding drinks.

It wasn't an unfamiliar environment for a girl who had done many things to survive, but if the Sienna from years ago, the little princess of Cosa Nostra, had seen it for the first time, she would have blushed with embarrassment.

That wasn't the case; I just moved on.

I felt my heart almost stop when I saw Dominic and Giovanni talking, both without masks. Enrico's sister had told me that Kiara, Giovanni's wife, was very curious about the club but too shy to imagine herself in such a place. So I hoped he'd be quite occupied showing her different things...

I was supposed to avoid the two bosses, and that was the plan between me and Enrico, but I couldn't resist. A daring streak pushed me to approach, eager to deceive those men who thought themselves so powerful and above the law.

"Good evening," I said, slightly altering my voice. "Where can I find the bathroom, please?" It was a phrase made up on the spot, something that came to mind.

Giovanni lifted his eyes to me, and I noticed he became suspicious. For a moment my blood ran cold, and I swore I would be caught. That he would start shouting for the soldiers surrounding the club to take me somewhere I would be tortured.

Fortunately, his suspicion faded, especially since Dominic, looking at his phone and not even glancing at me, pointed out the location, and I quickly headed for it before my boldness put me at risk.

I didn't know if the two would start discussing anything, and I didn't want to stick around to find out.

I headed toward the bathroom, although I didn't actually need to use it, but it became irrelevant the moment I saw him.

Fredericco Bonia. In an elegant suit, with his eyebrow piercing making him unmistakable. The mask he wore was something like the Phantom of the Opera, covering only one side of his face, so the jewel that distinguished him was on display. He was all smiles for a girl, but that didn't intimidate me. I changed my course, moving toward him, catching his attention.

He smiled back at me, and I knew, at that moment, that he hadn't recognized me.

"Wow!" he exclaimed, looking me up and down. "You're new here, aren't you? I don't remember seeing you before..."

I needed to stay firm. I needed to put aside the notion that this was one of the monsters living in my nightmares.

That was the idea: lure him in to strike. To become the bait so that he could be punished.

"Maybe it's the mask," I replied, with a sultry, almost whispered tone, over the music playing.

"Maybe it is..." He continued to smile. "Would you like a drink?"

"I didn't think anyone would offer me one," I said, sinuously, trying to be seductive, which had never been my trait.

"Because the luck was meant to be mine." Fredericco placed his hand on my back, and I had to control myself not to flinch at his touch. "Come with me, darling. I'll treat you the way you deserve to be treated."

Ah, I had no doubts about that, coming from a rapist.

I followed him, and we stopped in front of the bar. I received a drink, which I only pretended to sip, as I didn't want the alcohol to affect my judgment.

We started talking, and I had to embody the character. My luck was that the idiot was very talkative and began to open up about his life. He talked about what he did, without mentioning his position in the mafia, as that would never be allowed. I pretended to listen, smiling, laughing, and nodding when it seemed appropriate.

The party went on around us. People danced, and several girls performed, one after another. Drinks were constantly being served, and some were on the house. Many men and women were gambling, betting large sums, and I continued with the annoying Fredericco, hoping to seduce him to the point of falling into my trap.

We spent about an hour and a half in that charade until I spotted Enrico.

Dressed all in black, as always, his hair loose and swept to the side. The long overcoat didn't hide the shoulders that stood out beneath it, and he, like Dominic and Giovanni, wasn't wearing a mask. He watched me like a vigilant eagle, and I wondered how long he had been watching me from afar, ensuring I was safe.

I couldn't even imagine what he would do if he saw me in danger.

But I was fed up. So much so that I signaled to him, letting him know it was time.

Agreeing, Enrico moved away, and I could no longer see him.

With that in mind, I leaned toward Fredericco, whispering in his ear:

"Did you know I have VIP access? I got this invitation, you know? It was given to me by a gentleman, but I haven't seen him around. I suppose I could use it with someone else."

I took out the invitation that Deanna had managed to get for me and showed it to the idiot.

"Damn! You really do have access to the restricted area of the club. Only high-ranking people get something like this. I can already see it... You must be someone's lover, someone very powerful. Ungaretti, Caccini, one of the Cipriano boys, or the Preterotti... I'm well-served." He licked his lower lip, looking directly at my cleavage.

Son of a bitch!

"Why don't you come with me there? I think I'm curious about what's in those rooms."

"I'd love to show you."

We both got up, and he guided me, with his hand intertwined with mine, down a path leading to a staircase.

We ascended, and he used the invitation's barcode to open the door, allowing us to enter.

There was a corridor almost like a hotel, with closed doors, but some of them had glass with a curtain. Most of them were closed, and I didn't even want to imagine what went on behind them.

Fredericco was in front of me, and I swore he was going straight to the room indicated on my invitation, but he stopped abruptly, making me do the same.

"Look at this..." he whispered, as if we were two clandestine operatives. "I think the boss and his hot wife forgot to close a gap in the curtain."

It wasn't just a gap. It was more than that. Big enough for me to understand that Deanna had done it on purpose. She had said it would serve as a distraction, but I had no idea what Dominic thought about it, especially because he couldn't know the reasons behind her actions. I also knew, from what she had told me, that the owner of the place had an even more private room, which was obviously not on that floor. Everything was calculated.

Maybe she told her husband she wanted to show off a bit. Who knows...

Fredericco positioned me in front of him, not as hidden as would be prudent, but it was possible to see everything happening inside.

"Look at this deliciousness... Shall we watch for a while?"

I wanted to say no. Not only because it wasn't right to be a voyeur of a couple who hadn't given me permission to do so, but also because from what I could see, it wasn't the kind of sex that I thought would make me comfortable.

Deanna was naked, blindfolded, standing, wearing a collar around her neck. Dominic had pulled her, fastening the accessory to a metal bar, which looked very similar to those used by the girls to dance downstairs.

He wasn't gentle. He was rough, as if he were punishing Deanna for something. In the same manner, with the same look of anger, he grabbed her wrists, pinning them behind her back and the bar. I could see her chest rising and falling with each movement he made.

And he didn't stop there. With strips of leather that seemed made for this purpose, like belts, Dominic also fastened Deanna's waist to the bar, making her even more vulnerable.

It should have given me some kind of agony because Deanna was completely defenseless. Dominic was a huge man, shirtless, and she didn't seem frightened at all. Not even when he fastened something to her nipples, with a small chain hanging between them, linking one to the other. Her expression was one of pure pleasure.

Dominic took her face in his hands and kissed her in a surprisingly tender way, which contradicted my theory that he was punishing or trying to hurt her.

He whispered something in her ear, which I couldn't hear through the walls but made her shudder. He started to move his mouth down her neck while one of his hands circled her breast, which was pressed by the clamp. It must have been too sensitive because the moment he got closer, Deanna seemed to scream – at least from what I could see from her mouth's movement. And it didn't seem to be in pain.

How was it possible for a woman to feel pleasure that way? And why was I excited and curious about that kind of stimulation?

I could perfectly imagine how it would be if Enrico did one of those things to me. Would it remind me of the past, or would I trust the man I was with completely? Deanna didn't have traumas like mine, although she too had suffered some form of violence when kidnapped, but she seemed free. Surrendered. Aware of her body and everything her husband could offer her.

Dominic made her spread her legs, and he put his hand between them, playing with her clitoris. I couldn't see exactly everything he was doing to her because Dominic's body was quite large, and Deanna was very small, which made him almost completely cover her.

I was almost hypnotized, in a mix of confusing, completely incomprehensible, and new emotions.

I would have continued watching them for a while, even knowing it was wrong, until I saw Fredericco pulling out his phone, pointing the camera.

That outraged me.

"What are you going to do?" I asked, trying to stop him.

"Film, of course. Imagine how much I could blackmail Dominic Ungaretti with a recording like this, if necessary? Besides, I enjoy filming these things."

I couldn't allow it. It was already too much that we were there, watching a couple having sex; that that idiot was dry-humping Deanna's body.

Even though it distressed me, I placed my hand on his chest, pushing him and positioning myself in front of him, with our faces close.

"I'm so horny" I said, hoping to sound convincing. "Why don't you just take me to the room? I want to moan just like her."

That seemed to convince him, because he lowered his phone and smiled.

"Whatever you want, mysterious blonde."

He tried to kiss me, but I moved away, pretending it was a joke. Excited, Fredericco took my hand and started guiding me to the door with the number on the invitation.

Door 12.

The idiot had no idea what awaited him...

## CHAPTER THIRTY

### Enrico

The door opened, bringing her laughter. It was a rare sound that should have been appreciated in other situations, not shared with a son of a bitch like that.

It only served to make me even more pissed off.

Hidden in a corner of the room where I wouldn't be seen, I stayed on alert. I didn't fully trust the plan, even though I agreed it was a good one. If it weren't for Sienna putting herself at risk, I would have been inside without a second thought. Things changed a bit when it came to the woman I loved.

If the bastard touched her with even a single finger, he would die right there.

It was a torture to watch Sienna playing the Femme Fatale, pushing the idiot onto the bed and locking the door, just as we had planned.

"Stay there," she ordered, with a finger raised, and he obeyed.

How could he not? Anyone would kneel for a woman like her.

With her full hips swaying, she went to the sideboard, as agreed. She needed to pour a glass of whiskey for the guy and put in a sleeping pill to make him sleep like a lamb. The rest was up to me.

Deanna had reserved a room for us with an exit to the back of the house. The car was parked right outside. No one was going to stop us. Everything was orchestrated.

"With or without ice?" Sienna asked in a purring voice that made my insides twist.

"Without."

She served the drink and took it to him, handing it over. The idiot took a sip.

"Aren't you going to take off the mask, beautiful? I wanted to see that pretty face."

"Relax. We have time. Don't you think the suspense is sexy?"

"Of course it is. But I want to see if the top is as perfect as the bottom."

I gripped my gun, feeling ready to blow the bastard's brains out. The tone he used was lecherous, filthy. I could see his eyes because he was facing him from the point where I was hidden, and he was licking his lips, drooling over her.

For *my* woman.

He was the one who had hurt her. But I was going to hurt him much more for even looking at her with such desire.

"Maybe you don't even find me that pretty, you know? Maybe you already know me... The world we live in is so small, don't you think?"

Sienna was doing much better than I had imagined. Not that I doubted her. I always knew she was brave, with a will of iron. But amid the chaos that was probably reigning in her mind, facing her rapist, she had grown even stronger.

I admired her in a way that was impossible to put into words.

"How? Do I know you?" He reached out to touch her face, but Sienna held his hand back.

She mounted the man on the bed, doing things that hadn't been planned. She pulled out a pair of handcuffs from the drawer, fastening him to the bed. He was definitely excited.

"You really got inspired by the boss, didn't you? But look... it's the other way around. I was supposed to be doing this to you."

I saw Fredericco blinking several times, which confirmed that he was starting to get sleepy.

With Sienna's back to me, I only saw her reach for the wig, slowly removing it and letting her long, red hair fall loose. Fredericco was surprised.

Then she took off the mask, throwing it on the floor.

"Remember me?" she sounded vengeful. Even more so when the son of a bitch screamed, scared.

"You're dead! You're a fucking ghost!"

Sienna lifted one of her legs and revealed that she was wearing a garter with a knife attached to it. Another surprise for me. We hadn't planned any of that. She was on her own, shaping her revenge.

The knife ended up at Fredericco's throat. I could swear he was shitting himself in fear.

"What are you doing, girl? Why?"

"I should cut off your balls, you know? But I'll leave that to someone who can do a better job than this."

With her free hand, she signaled for me, and then I appeared.

Looking at me, Fredericco became even more terrified.

"I'm sure you've heard of Enrico Preterotti's reputation, haven't you? Do you know what he's going to do?" Sienna gave a little laugh, then leaned over the man to whisper in his ear: "He's going to finish you off and there won't be a single piece left to tell the tale."

I stared intensely at the man, serious, with my arms crossed, backing up what Sienna said. I would never contradict her. Whatever she wanted me to do with the bastard, all she had to do was ask. Her wishes were commands.

I watched Fredericco struggle against sleep as he thrashed around, but it was stronger than he was. In moments, he was out cold.

Then Sienna surrendered.

She got off him, staggering so disoriented that she bumped into me; her back colliding with my chest. I held her arms, steadying her, and turned her towards me.

"You were amazing, I hope you know that."

Her jaw clenched, and her lips trembled, but I had never seen anyone so purposeful, so determined. What an incredible woman.

"I know I was. He didn't defeat me..."

"No, sweetheart... He didn't." I used one of my hands to caress her face, losing a few moments in that gesture.

Sienna swallowed hard, and I stepped back, ready to put the rest of the plan into action.

She removed the handcuffs, freeing Fredericco, and I dragged him off the bed, tossing him over my shoulders, using the exit Deanna had shown us.

From that moment on, Sienna's nightmare was in my hands.

And then I would become his nightmare too.

# CHAPTER THIRTY-ONE

## Sienna

I swung my arm, slapping the man's face with all my strength. It was the first time I had ever physically assaulted someone like that, and I always swore it would feel horrible, because hurting someone wasn't in my nature, but all I felt was pleasure.

Power.

That bastard had taken so much from me that I wanted to take as much as I could from him in return.

If Enrico didn't kill him, which I doubted, I wanted him to never forget that moment. That every time he heard my name or remembered my face, he would think of all the suffering he endured that day.

Enrico didn't intervene this time. It was clear he wasn't at all pleased with my decision, but he respected my wishes.

Fredericco Bonia jolted awake from his induced sleep, almost jumping out of the chair. He would have jumped, in fact, if he hadn't been tied to the chair.

Seeing himself in this situation made him start to tremble.

"You can't do this! You're messing with the wrong person!" he shouted, visibly terrified.

"The line between what we can and cannot do is quite thin. I couldn't rape myself, could I? Agree with me?" My voice had never sounded so psychotic, and I feared what might come of that night. Something inside me would break once more, no doubt.

"I was drunk! It was your brother who incited me. It's his fault... I didn't want to..." He paused as Enrico, calm, grim, and silent, approached. He wore only a black button-up shirt, some buttons undone, revealing his muscular chest, along with black pants. His rolled-up sleeves left no doubt he was ready to get to work, as was his hair tied up in a bun.

The idiot was terrified of him.

"No, Enrico... you have to understand. She isn't normally beautiful. Who wouldn't want to get their hands on her? You surely understand... you're a man too."

Enrico said nothing. His face showed not a single expression. He looked like a dark ghost as he crouched and used a tool to crush one of the prisoner's toes.

Fredericco howled in pain, and I clenched my jaw, struggling not to close my eyes. I couldn't. I wanted to see.

"I believe you know what happened to her after everything, don't you?" Enrico began to speak. If I had once found his voice smooth and gentle, at that moment I came to fear it. He remained in full control, serene, but was clearly the messenger of chaos and pain.

"I know... I know..." Fredericco gasped.

"I believe you also know she has nothing to do with the whole mess, right?" The man nodded eagerly. "And how will you help us prove that? How will you spare yourself and help us?"

I looked at Enrico, knowing he had no intention of sparing Fredericco. He wouldn't leave there alive that night, but if he thought he had a chance, he might cooperate.

"I have a video... It's saved on my drive. It's from that night! I record everything! I recorded those bastards talking... I recorded us... us with her..."

He had a video! A video of my rape!

And why wouldn't he? If Fredericco wanted to film Dominic and Deanna in an intimate moment, why wouldn't he have done it more times?

The moment he revealed this, Enrico turned to me, and for the first time in the last few hours, I saw some kind of emotion on his face. He was concerned about me.

No wonder. I felt as if a knife had been driven into my chest. That violence I endured was now eternalized. Someone had watched it more than once, or could watch it. My agony, my despair... someone had enjoyed it.

I felt myself shudder, but I clenched my fist, hoping it would keep me as in control as possible.

That revelation stirred a very wild side of me. I took a dagger that Enrico had left with me and approached, stabbing it into his thigh and twisting the blade, making him scream again. I placed both hands on his shoulder, leaning close to his face so he could look into my eyes.

"What's on that recording?"

"There are people. T-there are... there are the guys. They were involved in e-everything..." he whined. "They talked about their plans. A-against the... against the Cosa Nostra."

"Why did you film it?" Enrico asked.

"I record everything. N-never know when I'll need it." He screamed as Enrico took the dagger, removing it and mimicking my action on the other thigh. He was stronger and did it with more violence. "I'm talking! I-I'm cooperating. *By God!*"

"Your God has abandoned you, *compagno*" Enrico said, with a terrifyingly menacing look, in a whisper. Then he leaned in, whispering in the prisoner's ear: "I'm your devil now."

Again, I heard a scream from the depths of Fredericco's throat, and I continued to watch as one of his fingers was mangled.

The torture session lasted a good few hours, and Fredericco was left nearly dead. Enrico knew he would die from bleeding and pain in that isolated place he had been taken.

As he continued to slump over the chair, unconscious after enduring more than anyone could, we took the phone and accessed his drive, using the fingerprint – one of the remaining ones.

I didn't want to look, but Enrico seemed to find what was needed. He sent the evidence to his email, making sure everything had been received correctly.

Satisfied, he threw the phone on the ground, shattering it, and grabbed a gallon of gasoline, pouring it all over the warehouse where we were and mainly on the man's body. He was unconscious, but as soon as the match was struck and the flames began to consume him, I was jolted again by a guttural, animalistic scream.

We left the warehouse hand in hand, and as soon as we were outside, amidst a vegetation that was almost a small forest, I bent over, surrendering to my own vulnerability, vomiting. Emptying all the agony out.

I felt Enrico's hand on my shoulder, gentle in a way I never could have imagined the man who acted inside that warehouse could be.

"Are you okay?" he asked, concerned.

"I think so. I'm not going to blame myself for faltering like this."

"No, you shouldn't."

I straightened up, taking a deep breath and tucking my hair behind my ear.

"What can we do with this footage?" I asked Enrico.

"First of all, we need to talk to Giovanni and Dominic. We'll clear your name with them." He paused, looking at me with seriousness. "I have a few more ideas, but I don't want to discuss them here. Shall we head to the hotel?"

I nodded, and he escorted me to the car.

I glanced over my shoulder, thinking about the destruction we had left behind.

And that was just the beginning.

## CHAPTER THIRTY-TWO

## Enrico

I stepped out of the shower and put on some uncomfortable clothes, since I planned to invite her to dinner, using some sort of disguise, right there in the hotel. I figured I'd have trouble sleeping without first wrestling with insomnia, tossing and turning in bed, just like I had.

I swore I would find her lying down at least, but she was sitting in a chair, all curled up, staring out the window.

We were on the top floor of a hotel in Manhattan, and the view was of the concrete jungle that made up New York. The lights blended with the starlight, creating a kind of blurry optical illusion.

"How are you?" I asked, approaching and standing in front of her chair.

She was hugging her knees, looking much more fragile than the woman I had seen act with all the skill and cruelty against her tormentor.

"Surviving," she replied with a sad smile.

That hurt me so much that I knelt in front of her, which seemed reasonably fitting for the situation.

"I don't want you to think that what I'm about to do is to make up for something, okay? And I also want you to consider that it's an effective way to keep you safe so we can reveal to everyone that you're alive."

Sienna remained silent, just looking at me, trying to understand where I was going with this. I reached into my pocket and pulled out a small box. Inside it, when I opened it, she found a ring with a huge diamond surrounded by red stones. The color it represented for me, because of her nickname.

"Enrico?" she exclaimed, surprised.

"Regardless of everything that's happening, marrying you is something I've wanted for a long time. Since I understood that I needed to become someone's husband. Since I realized that you could be mine."

"I guess you already know that I am, indeed, yours. I would never allow anyone to touch me the way you did. I'd never trust anyone else for that."

"I'm honored by that. To have your trust." I took the ring from the box, holding it between two of my fingers, examining it. "I want you to know that this will only be a symbol. My last name next to yours, just like the paper we'll sign. To me, you are the only woman. I don't need you to be my wife to know that I want to and will be loyal to you, not just as a husband should be to his wife, but as one person can be to another, in any circumstance."

I saw Sienna's eyes well up with tears, and she smiled. I wanted to believe it was a sign that she would accept, but she remained silent.

"So? Will you marry me? I know I'm not the perfect man you deserve; but I..."

I couldn't finish my sentence because she placed both hands on my face and pulled me towards her, pressing her lips against mine and kissing me. It wasn't a deep contact, but it was long, sweet, and very meaningful.

When we pulled away, I placed the ring on her finger, trying to control my emotions. I wasn't a man of outbursts, but the urge I felt was to pull her up, lift her off the ground, and spin around, celebrating a moment that was much more special than I could describe.

"Don't say that you're not the man I deserve, Rico. You are..."

"A monster," I completed. "You saw today. You witnessed everything I didn't want you to see."

"I'm no better. I'm broken. Like I'm defective."

I wanted to reprimand her for speaking such nonsense, but I just watched her, thinking there was a slightly better way to show her that she was completely wrong.

I stood up and extended my hand, waiting for her to do the same. When I felt her palm against mine, I pulled her towards a full-length mirror in the corner of the room, near the bed. I untied the robe I was wearing, taking it off and throwing it over a nearby armchair, leaving her in just a silk nightgown, an ivory tone with slight lace details. It barely covered her legs, had a generous neckline, and made her even more tempting.

I stood right behind her, wrapping my arms around her, resting my head on her shoulder.

"Look at yourself, *Scarlatta*. What do you see?"

She sighed, shivering in my arms.

"Chaos."

"No. You're wrong. If I said you weren't the most beautiful woman I've ever seen, I'd be lying. I know you don't like being associated with your beauty because it has brought you more bad than good, but there's so much more to you. I see strength, a great sense of justice, determination, kindness, balance, and a courage that few share."

"I don't..."

I held her tighter against me, making her lose the look of surprise.

"Don't say anything against that. It's the truth."

"You make me feel this way."

"You would discover all this on your own, my love. But I'll be here when you need me to reaffirm it."

Sienna's body relaxed more, and I attempted a bold move. I placed one hand on her breast, knowing that the silk of the nightgown would create friction and make the touch more sensitive. I used my nail to scratch her nipple, which made her squirm.

The other arm coiled around her like a serpent, but I was careful, not wanting to scare her. However, the way she reacted surprised me.

"I already asked, don't treat me like I'm made of porcelain. I saw things today at Dominic's club and I was..." she hesitated.

"You were what?" My voice sounded breathless as I whispered in her ear, still touching her and stimulating her nipples over the fabric.

"Turned on."

"Things like what?"

"Brutality. Domination. I should have felt disgust, fear..."

"No, darling. There's nothing wrong with that. What do you want me to do with you? Just ask and I'll give it to you."

I slid my hand lower, pressing on specific points of her flesh, reaching between her legs. The nightgown was so short that I had no trouble bypassing the barrier and finding her panties, pulling them aside and touching her clitoris, which made her moan softly, tilting her head on my shoulder.

At the same time, I tightened my other arm around her, since she had felt aroused by a bit of brutality.

"Don't take your eyes off the mirror, Sienna, and keep giving me instructions on what you want. Speak, describe." It would be my undoing. Hearing her talk about sex would undoubtedly destroy me and set me on fire very quickly.

My cock was already very hard inside my pants.

"I want you to pull my hair while you kiss my neck," she requested timidly, with a husky voice, which made me react in a very wild way.

I did as she asked, grabbing all her hair and twisting it in my fist, pulling her head back forcefully. My hand remained on her clitoris and my lips took over the piece of skin the nightgown didn't cover, descending along the curve from her neck to her shoulder.

"What else, Sienna?" I asked between kisses.

"I want you to put your finger inside me. Masturbate me."

"As long as you keep watching the mirror..."

"I will watch."

I moved my hand, letting it go behind her back but penetrating her deliciously wet pussy with two fingers. She gasped deeply and let out a moan. I couldn't resist and stopped kissing her, pulling her hair a little more and watching her expression in the mirror.

In the next thrust, I watched her moan a bit louder, opening her red heart-shaped lips. She also arched her body forward as much as she could, as if she wanted me to go even deeper.

"Rico..." My nickname escaped in a moan as well.

"What else, Scarlatta? I'm so fucking hard hearing you guide me."

"I want you to put your mouth on my breast while you masturbate me. I want you to suck it hard." Hearing her say that, I thrust into her wet slit with a bit more fervor.

"How rough?"

"Very..."

I stopped touching her and ripped the nightgown over her head, throwing it to the floor. I removed the belt from the waistband of my pants, wrapping it around her body, pulling it towards mine, making her my captive. As she had asked, I plunged my mouth onto her nipple, sucking it as if I wanted to devour it, licking, biting, and using my teeth to scratch it.

I held each side of the belt more tightly, gripping them in my fists like daggers. If I could bring Sienna inside me at that moment, I would have, because no closeness seemed enough.

Using the belt, I pulled her towards the bed, throwing her down but in a way that we were still facing the mirror. I took off my overcoat and shirt, leaving only my pants.

"Why are you all dressed up? I thought we were going to sleep."

"The idea was to take you to dinner, even if it was here at the hotel. But I guess we found something better to do."

"We definitely did."

I finished undressing and turned her over on the bed, putting her on all fours. I held her face and turned it towards the mirror, positioning myself behind her, using my fingers again to penetrate her.

"Keep watching. Tell me how you want me to masturbate you. Like this?" I thrust quickly, going in and out, but not too deep, with only my middle finger. "Or like this?" I went deeper and deeper, adding my index finger as well, hooking them to reach a spot I had already noticed was very sensitive.

"Like this. Deeper," she said amid moans, so I followed her request.

I grabbed her hair again, as I had before, making her arch her head back.

Suddenly, taking advantage of her having closed her eyes for a few moments, I swapped my fingers for my cock because I needed to calm my desire a bit.

She screamed as she felt it, and I didn't hold back, thrusting in a heavy, forceful rhythm.

"Mine. You're mine, Scarlatta. Only I can make your body react like this, can't I?"

"O-only you."

"Then tell me, how do you want me to fuck you?"

"Harder, Enrico. Harder."

Grabbing her hips with my free hand, I moved her back and forth, making our bodies collide in a way that made the bed creak.

I noticed Sienna was about to come by the way her body tensed, so I turned her over, placing her on her back, and used the belt that had fallen on the bed to bind her ankles together. I used all the brutality she had asked for, but with caution, trying to see if she was scared.

But no, she seemed very well.

With her legs completely together, I held them stretched up, at a ninety-degree angle with her body, and continued to fuck her, almost delirious from how tight she was in that position.

Sienna also seemed to approve because she let out a very loud scream the moment I forcefully entered her again, thrusting roughly.

It didn't take much more for her to come, and then I followed her, determined to give her more and more moments of pleasure like that.

She would never deprive herself again. I would never allow anyone to hurt her again, in any way.

# CHAPTER THIRTY-THREE

## Sienna

All I wanted was to go back to our cabin. I would be content to live in solitude for the rest of my life, with Lestat – whom I was eager to return to, but who was being well cared for by a caretaker hired by Enrico – my books, and my peace.

At the same time, I looked at the ring Enrico had placed on my finger two days ago and thought that it was the right thing: seeking my redemption, finding my place in that world, seeking justice, and marrying the man I loved.

I knew it was a difficult choice because Enrico couldn't leave everything behind. He had his responsibilities with the Cosa Nostra; he was the heir to one of the most powerful families, and I couldn't ask him to disappear, to run away and forget everything, leaving everything behind.

I couldn't ask, because I knew he would find a way to fulfill the whim.

So there I was: dressed in a beautiful dark green outfit, contrasting with my hair – which had been left loose intentionally – waiting hidden in Dominic's house. I had entered while he wasn't there, surrounded by Deanna and Enrico, very early.

My newest and only friend had convinced Dominic to host a dinner at his house, taking advantage of the fact that Giovanni and Kiara were in town. It was also expected that Alessio would return with

Luna, to return the girl to her family with the utmost safety, as Pietro had been killed.

She had spent a month on a huge estate in Scotland with the biggest Don Juan of the Cosa Nostra. Would that girl come back intact? It wasn't a problem for me to analyze.

And I had many others, actually. That night, my life would be put on the table, like an open book. The two most powerful men I knew would learn everything I had been through, both of whom would be capable of anything to kill me – if they didn't already think I was dead.

"Are you sure?" Enrico asked me, entering the room where Deanna had placed me to wait.

Everything was set. We would wait for them to arrive, and Enrico would tell everyone the truth. Then he would show the video. Only then would I appear, when things were a little less heated.

Even with all of this, I could swear I was going to die from fear.

"Yes. It's a necessary evil."

Of course, I didn't want people to see me at the worst moment of my life, so an edit had been made to the video. I didn't want my misfortune to be rubbed in their faces, but it was one of the proofs of my innocence, so at least the beginning of the nightmare would be shown, especially because the conversation between my brother and the others would be there. Enrico had also managed to get Fredericco to say some things before he died, under torture – which might not convince many – but everything together had to count for something.

Enrico approached me, holding my face and giving me a kiss on the forehead.

"Ready?" he asked, still looking into my eyes with tenderness.

I nodded, swallowing hard.

There was no time for regrets. From that moment on, the game could turn in my favor or against me forever.

I left the room and positioned myself strategically near the living room, listening to the conversation. Initially, at the start of the meal, they talked about business. Deanna was actively participating, showing that Dominic talked openly with her about shipments, partnerships, and meetings. Kiara was a bit quieter – at least I couldn't hear her voice – but I knew Giovanni didn't underestimate her opinion either.

"Where is your brother, Enrico? He should have been here by now," Giovanni asked, and I could also hear the sound of their baby, who accompanied them.

"I haven't been able to reach him yet," Rico replied. We were waiting for Alessio to start the show, but apparently, he changed his mind: "I need to show you something, even without Alessio's presence. It's not the most pleasant footage, but I need you to understand that this is an attempt to prove the innocence of a person who was considered a traitor without even a fair trial."

Since I could only see them and not hear them, I couldn't determine their reactions. Next, I heard chairs being dragged, knowing that Deanna was helping us, setting up the equipment.

The sounds that reached my ears at first were just the conversations between those people. My brother, among them.

Hearing Bruno's voice made me shiver. No matter how much time passed, he would always terrify me. The others too.

They talked about everything I had previously told Enrico. The betrayal of the Cosa Nostra and the way they planned to target each of the most powerful families first, to then take their place and control everything.

Minutes later, the most terrifying sounds began.

Bruno seeing me, and them commenting that I would betray them – that alone should prove my innocence, but I wouldn't count on luck. My brother chasing me, grabbing me, and taking me to the bed.

Thank God, it stopped there, but it was enough for them to understand what I had suffered.

I was so nervous remembering the darkest moments of my life that I shivered and, clumsily, knocked over a vase. It shattered on the floor, scattering shards everywhere.

"What the hell was that?" Dominic questioned, with his powerful voice.

There was again the dragging of chairs, and I judged that they were getting up.

There was nothing left to do but leave my hiding place because it was only a matter of time before they found me.

As I approached, revealing my presence, the two men drew their weapons from their holsters, pointing them at me. Giovanni positioned himself in front of Kiara and the baby, using them as a shield, but Enrico did the same with me.

"What is this woman doing here? Wasn't she dead?" Giovanni asked through gritted teeth.

"Do I look dead to you?" I tried to sound in control, but the truth was I was trembling. Enrico was also armed, and one of his arms was positioned behind me, as if to shield me, fearing that one of them might shoot.

"Guys, calm down! Please! Didn't you just see the video?" Deanna intervened.

"I admit I didn't see anything, I couldn't take it, but I heard enough."

"What are you talking about, Kiara?" Giovanni turned to his wife, who spoke, placing a hand on her chest and looking distressed.

"It's not possible that you didn't understand, Giovanni! Sienna never betrayed us. It was her brother, that crazy one. Didn't you hear the conversation? She is innocent."

"As far as I know, that video could have been forged," Dominic replied, but he didn't seem as sure of what he was saying.

"Oh, give me a break, Dom!" Deanna said, rolling her eyes. "Don't make me ashamed of you."

"You helped with all of this, didn't you? That's why you were so eager for us to have this dinner!" The New York boss seemed very displeased.

"I helped. I knew everything, but not that long ago. I only discovered and agreed that we needed proof before telling you, because I figured, as stubborn as you are, you would act this way."

The interaction among them was making me even more nervous, to the point that I grabbed Enrico's arm, squeezing it. Not that I wanted protection, it wasn't that. I just needed to stay grounded in reality while all that chaos unfolded around me.

"Can someone explain everything from the beginning?" Giovanni seemed a bit more reasonable, even though I knew he was as lethal as Dominic.

"Are you going to let her speak?" Enrico growled. "Are you going to lower your weapon or shoot before we get her side of the story?"

"I'm not going to lower my weapon, but I will let her speak. And she has a lot to explain, but she will get the benefit of the doubt because of the video. If all that is real, I'm sorry." He seemed sincere.

And it was something I could accept. Not that I liked being under the barrel of a gun, but just the chance to speak had to be seized.

I stood up, as I didn't trust the vulnerability that sitting gave me. I crossed my arms in front of my body, letting go of Enrico, and began to speak as soon as Giovanni's baby was taken out of the room by the nanny who accompanied them.

I explained everything I knew – which wasn't much – and recounted everything that happened to me after Bruno started abusing me. I talked about my engagement to Giovanni, how scared I was and had to run away; where I ended up, my work, the auction, and how Enrico found me. I told about our small investigation and the "conversation" with Fredericco Bonia.

"So Bonia is dead?" Dominic asked, and I nodded. "I never liked the bastard anyway. What a disservice..."

I would have laughed at how Dominic spoke, but I wasn't in the mood for that. My fear wouldn't let me go much further. Speaking, staying on my feet, facing those people... and all while keeping my head up, because that's how I was taught to do it, was requiring a tremendous effort.

When I finished, I waited for them to give their opinions. Giovanni, Dominic, and Enrico still had their weapons in hand, but the two bosses no longer aimed them at me. In contrast, my Shadow Knight remained firm and strong, standing like a statue, ready to shoot and defend me if necessary.

"All this time, you were innocent?" Giovanni was the first to speak, with a furrowed brow, surprised.

"Yes. It was never my intention to betray the Cosa Nostra. I just wanted to get rid of my brother. I also didn't want Kiara to get hurt. She was the closest thing to a friend I could have, even though she probably didn't consider me one, since we never had a chance to get to know each other well."

"Did you agree to marry me to escape from Bruno?"

"Of course!" I exclaimed, almost hopeful that they would believe me. "I would marry anyone! It would be a much better fate than continuing to live with my brother."

"He was a monster!" Kiara shivered. "I believe you, Sienna. And I always wanted us to be friends. If you had told me what was happening..."

She couldn't do anything. She was as much a victim of the mafia as I was.

We were women trapped by our destinies. Still, I was grateful for the kindness.

Unexpectedly, even amid the pointed guns, Kiara came towards me, placing herself in front of me. Both her husband and her cousin moved, ready to do something and protect her if necessary. But she opened her arms and pulled me into a warm embrace that made my chest tighten.

"Welcome back, Sienna."

Over her shoulder, I saw the men relax a little, and Giovanni even put away his gun.

It was a truce. But for how long?

## CHAPTER THIRTY-FOUR

### Enrico

I still couldn't relax, knowing that Dominic and Giovanni could, at any moment, change their minds and corner Sienna, even after their wives were on our side.

Fortunately for me, there was another concern among us. Alessio had indeed not shown up and had not given any news.

Gathered in Dominic's dining room after we had eaten, still in a strange tension due to Sienna's presence – although Kiara and Deanna were making every effort to make her as comfortable as possible – I checked my phone for the umpteenth time, without success.

Dominic noticed.

"Your brother is going to cause us problems," he said in a stern tone.

I couldn't blame him. Alessio was unpredictable, impulsive, often immature. I wondered when the day would come that he would mature. At some point, he would need to take on a higher hierarchical position. If our father died and I took control of Los Angeles, I would want him by my side as consigliere, because there was no one in the world I trusted more, despite everything.

I wasn't sure if he was ready for that.

"I'm worried about the girl," Deanna said.

"Alessio would never harm her!" Kiara exclaimed confidently, receiving a withering look from Giovanni. I knew that the Chicago boss was jealous of my brother.

"No, he wouldn't," I confirmed.

"It depends on what you consider 'harm,'" Giovanni said. But then he turned to Sienna: "But while we try to find Alessio, I want you to know that we will make sure your abusers pay. Not just for conspiring against us. We would have the same attitude for hurting you."

I looked at Sienna, and if I knew her well, she was trying to control her emotions. Giovanni's attitude had certainly surprised her, but more than that, she was not alone. There were people fighting for her. It was no longer a silent struggle.

"Thank you," was all she managed to respond, then Kiara placed her hand over hers.

"We're with you, dear." The two smiled at each other.

"How do you plan to make people know? Not everyone will give her a chance to explain herself like we did," Dominic spoke up.

"We're getting married." They probably had already seen the ring on Sienna's finger, but it was good to state it. Not just because I wanted them to know, but because I liked to think that soon she would be my wife. "With the protection of my surname, things might get a little less complicated."

"She will have our support," Giovanni promised, and would have said more if my phone hadn't rung.

To my surprise, it was Alessio. On a video call.

I answered quickly, almost fearing what I would find out.

"Buona sera, fratello," he greeted me from the other side of the line, wishing me good evening, and looked more serious than ever.

"Alessio? What happened to you? We were supposed to meet at Dominic's house tonight. The Ciprianos are waiting for our call!" I tried to stay calm, because obviously something was wrong.

"I know." Alessio sighed, and I almost didn't recognize my usually playful and immature brother's demeanor. "I'm not giving her back, Enrico. Not until we're married."

I was quite shocked, and I realized that the others around me were too. Being a video call, of course it wasn't a private conversation, and I suspected that was exactly Alessio's intention.

"What are you talking about?"

"I spoke with Mattia Cipriano. Now that he's taking on the position of head of Texas, he decided that I'm not a good choice as Luna's husband. He wants to marry her to the oldest of the Pellegrinis."

"The man is about fifty years old," Dominic said.

The Pellegrini boss was already seventy-nine years old, with failing health. It was more than likely that Luigi Pellegrini, his eldest son, would take over.

He had been married once before, and his wife had died under very suspicious circumstances. Not to mention that we had seen her covered in bruises several times.

I understood Alessio. I wouldn't have the courage to give the girl back either, if that was her fate.

"Do you understand now? If I can convince them to let me marry her, at least I'll be able to protect her."

Alessio was too desperate for someone who just wanted to help a beautiful young woman in trouble.

"Have you fallen in love?" I asked bluntly.

The moment Alessio hesitated, remaining silent for a few moments, I was certain of what the answer would be.

"It seems so. We won't go back until we convince her brother."

"You can get married without his permission too. You're in Scotland," Dominic said again.

"She doesn't want to. You don't know Luna... she's a girl... God, she's so innocent! So proper," Alessio really sounded very much in love. It could be a fleeting thing, just because my brother was very susceptible, but he cared about the girl. Enough to even want to *marry* her.

"We'll help you, Alessio," Deanna said, receiving a stern look from Dominic, which she didn't care about at all. "Stay strong over there."

"*Grazie, sorellina.*"

"Anyway, I think it's a good idea for you to go back with her and let your father handle the negotiations," Giovanni opined.

"He won't want to get involved in this."

"It's a good marriage. I don't think he'll oppose it," I replied to my brother, because even though he was closer to our father, I knew him better.

"And my mother is there to convince him."

Deanna was right. It was hard to imagine Massimo Preterotti denying anything to Cássia. That could definitely be a trump card for us.

"Thank you. It's good to have you on my side."

"Yes, we are... but the truth is, you won't come to my wedding, will you?" I threw out the information without much preparation.

It might be silly of me, because I wasn't that kind of person, but thinking about the word "wedding" associated with Sienna honestly made my heart light; almost as if there was salvation for me amidst the shadows.

"Wedding? What do you mean, Rico?"

Yeah, I had a lot to tell him. So I needed to start from the beginning...

# CHAPTER THIRTY-FIVE

## Enrico

It wasn't the wedding I wanted to give her. It wasn't the triumphant entrance she deserved as a bride; no beautiful dress, no packed church, not even a party. Still, the people who mattered were present, even Alessio managed to show up with his Luna, since we decided to hold our ceremony at the cabin, isolated from everything and everyone, on the lake, with a minister to officiate and make everything official.

Sienna wore a dress that Kiara had in her atelier; a beautiful piece that hugged her body like a mermaid, white, full of lace, and a neckline that exposed her shoulders. We managed to get a bouquet and set up a tent to make everything reasonably romantic.

Even Lestat was present.

I was moved when I saw her walking towards me, alone, illuminated as if made of light.

When it was declared that she was mine and we could sign, and I saw Sienna Preterotti written for the first time, I had to take a deep breath. When I kissed her, knowing she had become my wife, the feeling was different.

No one would stay with us for long, as they planned to leave us alone, but we opened a champagne to celebrate and toasted. Despite everything, all the obstacles that led us here, when I intertwined my arm with Sienna's, to taste our glasses, her eyes were misty, full of emotion.

The ice queen even managed to smile.

And if I was able to evoke that feeling in her, nothing else mattered. We would fight until the end to make it last forever.

With that thought, shortly after, I received my father by my side. I had told him everything in the most superficial way possible, but Dominic and Giovanni had a private meeting among the bosses and contained the outburst he caused.

"You're marrying a complicated woman, Enrico. I confess it wasn't the fate I wished for you," he said, holding his glass, very formally.

That's how we treated each other. He was much more accessible to Alessio, and I understood that he was the second son he could pamper differently. He didn't need to turn him into the soldier I was meant to be one day.

Not that I respected the kid, because I always said he had gone off the rails, but the treatment between us was very different.

"It wasn't the fate I wished for *her*. But I don't think you understand that, being a man who kidnapped his own daughter and forced her to marry."

My father took a deep breath. He didn't take criticism well, but I couldn't help but speak.

"Deanna is fine."

"It was luck. It could have gone wrong."

"That's beside the point, Enrico. I'm handing over my heir to a woman who, as far as we know, is innocent but could surprise us and pull the rug out from under us. The story is convincing, but..."

"There are no *buts*," I vociferated. "I trust her and think she deserves an apology. Now Sienna is my wife, and you owe her respect."

My father nodded, which surprised me. He was agreeing and admitting his fault.

"Do you know how you're going to reveal the truth?"

"Sienna is willing to let us show the edited video, the same one we used with Giovanni and Dominic."

"Will you allow your wife to be exposed like that?"

"I don't have to allow anything. It's her choice. But above all, it might ensure her survival."

He took a deep breath and put one hand to his head.

"She has significant support. Three of the bosses are willing to help her, but the choice your brother made regarding Cipriano could be complicated."

"Will you support him?"

"What do I have left? Go to war with my son? An imprudent kid can be very dangerous. But a passionate one is much worse. Besides, it's not a marriage I dislike, especially since it had already been negotiated with her father."

I cast a glance in Luna's direction, with the women, and she still looked like a very frightened little creature among strangers. But that only lasted until my brother approached, with a glass of juice, treating her as if she were the most precious thing he could find.

The girl then opened a huge smile and looked at him as if he were her hero, her knight in shining armor.

It had all the potential to go wrong, but who was I to judge them?

"I hope you are happy, son," my father suddenly said, breaking the silence. He put his hand on my shoulder, not with much tenderness, but it was as close to a fatherly gesture as I could imagine from him towards me.

With that, he stepped away, approaching Deanna and Cássia, who were talking.

People stayed with us for a few more hours, but when they left, I found Sienna still in her beautiful dress, facing the lake, looking like a melancholic painting. I positioned myself behind her, watching her heavy curls curl at the ends, with two sections pinned with flowers, coming together at the back. She looked like a princess.

I hugged her around the waist, keeping myself behind her, and she was surprised by my presence.

"I didn't mean to scare you."

"You didn't scare me. I was just a bit lost."
"Sad?"
"No! How could I be?"
I shrugged.
"I don't know. I still think it's a distant dream that you agreed to marry me."
"Don't be silly and dramatic, because it doesn't suit you. I've been in love with you for years, but over time I had to push those feelings aside. Nothing has changed."
I tightened my arms a bit more around her.
"So why do you look so thoughtful?"
"It's just that we still have a long way to go, right? And what if people don't accept my version of events?"
I turned her to face me, making her look into my eyes.
"They will accept it. But I suppose those should be thoughts for another night. Another time."
"Of course... I'm sorry. It's our wedding night."
"Yes, Scarlatta... it is," I whispered, placing my hands on her face and touching her lips.
The kiss was slow, but I sought her mouth the way I wanted, unable to contain myself, demanding what could be demanded and giving all of myself in return.
I leaned in and picked her up, as the bride she was, carrying her into the cabin.
I didn't want to think about anything else that night, other than how much I wanted to pleasure my wife. How much I wanted her to be mine, not just on paper but with her soul, body, and heart.

## Sienna

ENRICO CARRIED ME UP the stairs in his arms. He walked slowly, never letting his eyes stray from mine, and I could read a million promises in each of them, in the depth of the blue hue they held. They seemed even darker as he looked at me.

Instead of laying me on the bed, he left me standing, with my back to him.

There were countless buttons on the back of my dress, even with a plunging neckline that nearly dipped to the curve of my butt, adding volume. I had sworn he would be romantic, given it was our wedding night, and although that wasn't disappointing, I had liked the man I had met during the last times we made love, especially after the night at the hotel when I asked for more brutality.

But when he pushed me against the wall, pinning me there with his body, I gasped.

Enrico leaned in, kissing the exposed part of my back, letting his tongue trace the line they formed. He used his mouth to unbutton my dress slowly, with his teeth, while continuing to mark me with his lips, little by little.

When the dress was fully opened, Enrico took it off, letting it slide down my body, creating a white pool of fabric and lace at my feet. Keeping me in the same position, he also undressed himself, not giving me a chance to do it, grabbing my wrists and pressing them against the wall, making me flatten myself against it as he took his time kissing my shoulder, leaving a strong bite that made me moan softly.

"Did I hurt you?"

"No. It was... good."

"Great, because I want to mark you all over."

As soon as he said that, he pressed his hips forward, making his cock come into contact with my butt, showing me he was extremely excited, as hard as a rock.

He released one of my wrists and moved his hand to my butt, squeezing it and giving it a smack that I found surprisingly enjoyable. Then, while my skin was still burning, one of his fingers found my slit, playing with it, seeking entry, going after what I so wanted to give him.

He toyed with my clitoris using his thumb, and penetrated me with his middle finger, giving another bite to my back.

I felt him lowering himself, getting on his knees, while turning me around to face him.

"Only you, Sienna. Only you can make me feel this way, surrendering. I'm crazy about you. You know that, don't you?"

"Yes, Rico. I'm crazy about you too."

Grabbing my butt with both hands, I felt his mouth take the place of his fingers in a fervent oral sex that made me need to lean my back against the wall, or my legs would certainly not be able to support the weight of my desire.

He placed his tongue inside my pussy, sliding it from side to side, sucking forcefully. In one of his thrusts, I swore I would lose all my air from a moan, but I fought to breathe again, at least until Enrico used his tongue to play even more, making it quick, hot, and wet, tireless.

I could already feel all my muscles contracting when he suddenly stood up, lifting me off the ground and pressing me against the wall again, my legs wrapped around his waist.

With a few movements of his hips, he found the exact spot to penetrate me. First with caution, but soon with more intensity. I clung to his shoulders as his arms supported me by the thighs, also using his strength to lift my body and lower it, sliding along his cock, which was already well-lubricated by my excitement.

"Enrico! Oh, God..." I cried out, not only from pleasure, though that was very obvious, but because of how I always felt free while in his arms. He never inspired fear, insecurity, or unease. With Enrico—my husband from that moment on—I could only feel feminine, dominated, but in a positive way.

The scream I let out when the orgasm hit me, reaching me with force, was proportional to how my body leaned forward. Luckily, Enrico was holding me, because if it depended on my legs, I would never have been able to stand.

I swore I would lie on the bed, but he turned me, picking me up like a bride again, sitting with me on his lap, reaching between my legs with his fingers. My pussy was sensitive, so any touch would set it ablaze once more.

"Sienna Preterotti," he whispered, thrusting again. "You are all mine. No other man will touch you this way, will they?" Enrico continued to masturbate me, holding me tightly against him.

"No other... none."

"Tonight, I'm not letting you rest, Scarlatta. It will all be about your pleasure. Let's see how many times more you'll come."

I didn't take long to get there again. Not with that voice whispered and husky telling me those things, much less with his experienced hands touching me.

Barely recovered from the second orgasm, he finally laid me on the bed, but on my stomach, showing me how many different positions I could be taken by him.

It went on for hours and hours like that. Each time I came, the next seemed more intense because I was more susceptible, more vulnerable.

When he penetrated me again, thrusting with force, the sun was already rising on the horizon, showing that he had kept his promise to give me pleasure throughout the night.

Enrico also came, spilling inside me. We were both exhausted, drunk on each other, but we collapsed on the bed, facing each other, with eyes locked, filled with love. Neither of us could speak, and we didn't need to.

Silence was our witness. No matter how much we still had to fight. Together, we would always be stronger.

# CHAPTER THIRTY-SIX

## Enrico

One by one. That was our plan.

Before even showing people that Sienna was alive and trying to prove her innocence, we had scores to settle.

There had been five of them at first. Only three remained. Bruno was killed by Giovanni when he tried to kidnap Kiara. The other, Fredericco, met his end at my hands.

There was one left for each of us, since Giovanni and Dominic were going to help me, and Alessio was sorting out his issues with Luna. He was set to be marked, in fact, in a few days, for everyone to meet in person to discuss their wedding. Mattia hadn't refused, but he was still unsure if it was the best choice. So, our father would intervene.

At that moment, however, the last thing I wanted to deal with was my thoughts about my brother's married life. Mine was going very well, thank you, but I wanted to be with my wife. To show her off, to attend events with her, without anyone looking at her like she was a traitor.

We used Dominic's club again to capture them. VIP invitations were sent out, and we outlined almost the same strategy, using girls to lure them to the rooms, and there we knocked them out. This time, however, the bait wouldn't be our wives.

None of the three we captured were that important within the Cosa Nostra hierarchy. They were three associates who did their dirty work for the *famiglias* and had their business tied to us. However, all were heirs to fortunes. Spoiled rich kids who thought they could have everything they wanted. More than that, they surely believed they would benefit if other groups took over.

Unfortunately, their days were over.

We took the guys to a warehouse provided by Dominic, since we were in his city, and we faced them. All three. Arms crossed. When the first one woke up, he became agitated upon seeing us. Of course, he knew what that meant.

They were in deep shit.

"So? Enrico, will you do the honors? After all... it was your wife these sons of bitches touched," Dominic was taunting, but he didn't even need to. My blood was already hot enough.

I cast a glance at the prisoners. All of them with their arms bound to the chairs. Naked.

The second one also woke up. The third remained unconscious.

Lucky him.

"With pleasure," was my reply to Dominic before the chaos began.

There was nothing to uncover, no information to collect, just violence, but with a purpose. In the end, we weren't dealing with good people, but with rapists who had enjoyed at the expense of a girl who had become extremely traumatized.

Not to mention they were traitors, that was more than proven.

The blood shed was not innocent.

With that settled, our next step was to clear Sienna's name. And we didn't intend to do it timidly. It couldn't be, because letting the rumor spread would do no good, as a dead woman couldn't return to life without causing some disruption.

The legal issue would be resolved because we had our contacts. Nothing was impossible for us, especially when we didn't have to worry about the police, as they ignored us. It was a silent and very beneficial agreement for both sides.

We hoped things wouldn't become a whirlwind, not only because it was time for us to have some peace but also because Deanna had announced her pregnancy. Dominic was a bit paranoid about her and also stressed, already expecting that she wouldn't settle down or calm that restless soul.

He liked it, but when his heir was at stake, it was much more complicated.

The event was organized by our women. It wouldn't be such a grand party, but it would include the top of the hierarchy within the Cosa Nostra.

Sienna wanted something none of them would forget.

Once again using her faithful wig, along with makeup that made her face look slightly different, we prepared her. There were hired soldiers to protect and watch over her, and I didn't intend to leave her side.

She would also go on stage armed, with a bulletproof vest under the dress, which had to be a little looser because of it.

A whole structure was set up to ensure her protection. Still, I was tense.

It was one of those charity auctions that those people loved so much. A request from Sienna, for it to be something symbolic. She would be responsible for presenting it.

The stage was a setup in a renowned party hall in Manhattan. This would be another protection for Sienna, because with a very well-thought-out light show, her face wouldn't be highlighted. And it was very simple to see that people had immense difficulty seeing what they *didn't* want to see.

The beautiful and young Esposito heiress, in everyone's opinion, was dead and buried. One less problem in their perfect little lives. They judged the girl as a traitor, never giving her a chance to defend herself, but when cornered, they wouldn't have half of her courage.

I normally didn't like to participate in those auctions. At the last ones I attended, I left before they ended because I had Sienna to take care of. But even before she was under my protection, I was never a fan of what they probably considered as something to clear their consciences.

My demons wouldn't be exorcised with a public charity to make me look like a better citizen.

But that wasn't the focus here.

I went up on stage with Sienna, staying close while she, quite nervous, positioned herself in front of the podium, took the microphone, and began to speak.

The items to be auctioned were artworks and exclusive pieces, donated by Cosa Nostra members from their personal collections and resold for exorbitant prices. They made fifty percent, and the rest was donated to charity.

The first lot was presented. Sienna read the description and did as she was trained. She was immensely brave and held her head high, playing her role, breathing, and getting into character. She distributed smiles, showed herself to be charming, kind, and professional.

There were ten lots, and then the show would begin.

Just before the final item was auctioned for one hundred fifty-five thousand dollars, I glanced at the audience, seeing Dominic, Giovanni, and my father, all in place. Alessio wasn't there. We decided to settle that matter first before dealing with Luna's return to her family and the negotiation of their wedding, which would be discussed that same night, a little later.

I focused my attention on Sienna, watching her prepare for the final moment. She swallowed hard, lowered her head, hesitated, but then lifted it up like the warrior she was.

Her eyes sparkled with fire. The hand not holding the microphone was clenched on the podium, at the side, her knuckles white from the force she was applying.

"The next item, ladies and gentlemen, is the truth. I'd like to give it to you for free."

Everyone became a bit agitated, especially since the lively, smiling woman who had been entertaining them earlier had disappeared, replaced by a very serious, very anxious one.

"Some time ago, you turned a blind eye to what was happening to a girl. A daughter of the Cosa Nostra, whom you swore to protect and serve. That girl suffered under your own roof while her brother decided her future and abused her in her own bed, in the home she was supposed to consider sacred." Movement began, and I became even more alert. "That girl was deemed a traitor when the greatest nightmare of her life sold out to a senseless cause. She had to flee to survive because if she had stayed, no one would have given her a chance to explain. She wouldn't have had the right to a trial. But how could she side with those she hated most? How could she betray people when all she wanted was for those same people to remove that brother from her reach? She just wanted to be saved."

As soon as Sienna finished speaking, the big screen lit up, and some videos, which we had edited, began to play. We made sure to include all the content of the conversation between the bastards and Sienna's brother, discussing the betrayal plan against the organization, but cut some parts of the rape. We left it implied and didn't cut the audio, keeping the screen black.

The audience's reactions were varied. Disgust, despair, anger, shock. Some women covered their eyes; others seemed so anguished that they cried, even though nothing more terrifying had been exposed. Most of the men remained impassive. I had no doubt that some of them had already abused girls like Sienna.

But not all. Some looked revolted as well.

Then, the video of Fredericco emerged, in the middle of the torture session, revealing the truth. Although his testimony was biased, considering his state, his speech was quite believable. More than that, it didn't make sense for Sienna to be allied with her brother, except through sheer blackmail.

All the plans were detailed there, and now we knew. We could act.

I looked at Sienna again, and she was crying. I wanted to go to her and hold her, comforting her, but that would be a way to diminish her value. She didn't need me, not at that moment, because she was strong and brave enough to compose herself alone.

"I had to flee. To survive. I had to almost starve, do things I'm not proud of, and was auctioned off, just like these items you had the chance to bid on. If it weren't for Enrico Preterotti, I would be lost. Now I'm back, and I don't want your forgiveness. I just want my space, my right to live, and for my family's name to be cleared, even if my brother doesn't deserve it. My father and mother were not to blame for his cruelty. And neither was I."

With great care, Sienna removed her wig. At the same time, I approached her, as did Dominic, Giovanni, my father, and their women, who went up on stage, standing by her side, surrounding her to show that they were with her. It was a team of great power, no doubt.

"This girl is under our responsibility. Anyone who turns against her will be turning against us," Dominic said, but it wasn't even necessary. No one would be crazy enough to oppose them.

I knew Sienna would be safe. From that moment on, she would have her justice, which had been her wish from the start.

## CHAPTER THIRTY-SEVEN

### Enrico

My father and I exchanged impatient glances. It couldn't be that Alessio would fail again.

It was a small gathering—just me, my father, Mattia Cipriano, and a soldier on each side. There was no need for more than this because it was meant to be a friendly meeting. According to what had been discussed, Luna's brother was a bit reluctant to accept the idea of the marriage between our families, and he had even suggested me as a better option, but he was informed that I was no longer available.

My father was willing to use the worst card possible, but it might work—claiming that her reputation would be ruined after two months living in an isolated place with Alessio, who had the worst reputation when it came to women.

Not to mention that the two were in love.

"If your brother doesn't show up, he'll be on his own this time. I won't allow him to come and complain," my father grumbled, justifiably, but trying to make sure only I heard.

"He will come, *papá*," I said, not very convincingly, but hoping I was right.

The expression my father showed made me swear he didn't have much faith in what I believed. And I had to agree that if Alessio decided to maintain his stubbornness in not showing up so the girl could see her brother and things could be negotiated properly without stress and fights, it would be hard to defend his cause.

A few more moments of waiting passed until someone's arrival was announced. We were in an Italian restaurant in New York, owned by one of our associates. A place where many of our meetings took place because it was neutral enough to avoid involving families and to avoid being threatening.

I looked up and saw Alessio entering hand in hand with Luna. We all stood up from the table, and I saw the couple stop near us. The girl clung to my brother's arm, seeking his protection, and he pulled her closer.

"We're here," Alessio said, lifting his head with surprising determination.

Mattia moved from my side, approaching Luna and kissing her on the top of the head. Watching them, it wasn't hard to see the girl's body tense at her brother's touch.

"We understand your interest in marrying my sister, is that correct?" Mattia asked, and I saw Alessio straighten his shoulders.

"Where are your other brothers? As far as I know, the decision should be made by all of them, right?" my brother insisted, still firm. He knew something he hadn't shared with us.

Something that affected Luna beyond just marrying a much older and possibly aggressive man.

"My brothers have nothing to do with this," Mattia said very firmly, which also made me a bit uneasy.

There was a strange atmosphere in the air, something I only began to notice at that moment. The soldier assigned to stay alert by Mattia's side was overly tense, as if ready to act the moment he was ordered.

I decided to stay on high alert, although initially I thought it might just be paranoia.

"Of course they do. If it's Luna's marriage and your father is no longer alive, everyone can have a say. Including her."

Luna had another sister even younger than she was; a fifteen-year-old girl, whose fate I didn't even want to imagine.

"I'm the only one interested in this. Neither Lorenzo nor Giulio care about any of this. And Tizziana is just a child."

"Can we cut to the chase?" my father interrupted. "It doesn't matter who will resolve this matter, as long as it gets resolved. We're trusting that your family is still worth considering because it was agreed upon by members of the Cosa Nostra that your action in turning in your father was honorable enough to give you a chance."

Mattia smiled.

"If my family has a stain on its reputation, so do you. Look at who your son married."

Mattia wanted to provoke me, no doubt. In my mind, I imagined a million ways to go after him and beat him until he begged for mercy for mentioning Sienna that way. If the overwhelming majority of the members of the Cosa Nostra had accepted the story as true, no ordinary bastard would contest it.

I clenched my jaw and focused my eyes on him, with a promise that any misstep would be his sentence.

"Why do you think I should agree to this marriage? Don't you think my sister is worth more than a union with a clueless kid who contributes nothing and can't even see a skirt?"

Alessio stepped forward, placing Luna behind him.

"I'm willing to be a good husband to her. That should be enough," he said through gritted teeth.

"They're in love, Mattia. I don't think it's wrong to arrange a marriage that's not just about power interests."

Once again, the bastard gave a malicious laugh.

"You say that because your daughter married one of the most powerful men in the Cosa Nostra."

"And another died for it," my father replied with sorrow.

"Don't you think some people die in the name of a greater cause? Tonight, for example... We came to discuss a marriage, but things don't always go as we wish, do they?"

It was too late to act. On our side, I was probably the first to realize what was happening; that talk about a "greater cause," the fanatic expression on his face, the calculated movement.

Mattia reached for the holster on his vest.

He grabbed the revolver.

In an instant, he aimed at my father's forehead.

He fired.

Although I was trained to react in stressful moments, not to be affected by emotions, I found myself completely paralyzed.

Luna let out a scream at the sound of the gunshot, and my brother and I stood frozen, watching my father's eyes widen, his body go rigid and standing for a few moments, only to fall like a piece of wood a minute later.

"*Papá!*" Alessio shouted, taking a step towards him, trying to catch him before he fell to the ground.

Not that it would make any difference. My father was already dead.

"We have a greater cause. It's not personal. We'll see each other soon." I heard Mattia say and then run away, followed by his soldier.

I tried to act quickly, drawing my gun while hearing the sounds of Alessio crying with my father in his arms. I shot, hitting Mattia's soldier, who was right behind him. With the second shot, I hit the bastard, but he kept running.

Despite my good aim, he managed to get out of the restaurant and onto the street, leaving his man behind, sprawled on the ground bleeding out.

"*Papà!* No!!! *Papà!*"

My soldier, without needing any instruction, ran after Mattia, but I suspected he wouldn't catch him. That meeting had been orchestrated, planned to be my father's tomb.

"Enrico! Our father! What have I done? It's my fault! If I hadn't insisted on all this... If not..." Alessio began to say, his voice choked.

All I could do was cast a glance at Luna. She had both hands over her mouth, staring at my father's corpse.

It was her brother who had caused this; who had killed the father of the man she loved. The girl had lived in a convent for most of her life and then had to face death in this way. The scene was horrifying, and she would never forget it.

Nor what Alessio had said.

He blamed himself for our father's death. He blamed his love for that girl for the tragedy.

And it became even clearer when, shortly after the burial, my brother withdrew into a darkness that resembled my own. He didn't want to talk, seemed like a shadow of himself, and even decided to take Luna back to the convent, where he thought she would be safer.

Safer than with us or with her own family.

No one would ever be safe within the mafia. No matter how hard we tried.

My father's death was the greatest proof of that.

# CHAPTER THIRTY-EIGHT

## Sienna

Sitting in a high-backed chair, two months after his father's death—which was considered an acceptable mourning period—Enrico was receiving applause from the same Cosa Nostra members who had been present on the day it was revealed that I was alive.

The same people who had been reluctant to accept me back into their closed world were now applauding my husband for taking his rightful place as heir. From that moment on, Los Angeles was in his hands. It should have been an important moment, but Enrico was not happy. How could he be? The loss of his father had affected him deeply, but not more than it had affected Alessio.

He was close to his brother, attending what was considered a ceremony, waiting for his moment to be in the spotlight as well. Still, he seemed more serious than ever, waiting in a military position.

Just like me, with a desire for revenge, I began to dive into training to strengthen myself, just as Alessio was doing. He had been trained, as the mobster he was, but never as thoroughly as Enrico. Mattia was still at large, and although he said little about it, he intended to hunt down the traitor.

Young Lorenzo Cipriano had taken his brother's place, but everyone still looked down on the family. What had saved them was Mattia making it clear that they had absolutely nothing to do with his plans. It might have been a lie, but an investigation was underway, and so far, nothing had been proven.

However, that was not enough for Alessio to take Luna as his wife, which had been his intention from the beginning. We no longer knew anything about her, but I remembered her innocent face when she had said goodbye, ready to return to the convent after having her heart broken.

I didn't agree with my brother-in-law's attitude, but I couldn't judge him, as he was also suffering. If he was truly in love with the girl, he would end up regretting it at some point.

I just hoped it wouldn't be too late.

"Thank you all for the warm welcome," Enrico began to speak. I knew it was hard for him to make a speech, but it was a necessary evil. From that moment on, he would need to loosen up a bit more, as it would be his role to manage, organize, and oversee all the *famiglias* in Los Angeles. "I would like to say that this is a celebration, but unfortunately, it doesn't make me happy to be taking a place that my father occupied with such seriousness and responsibility for so many years."

Enrico lowered his head and swallowed hard.

His relationship with his father was not exactly the best, but he loved him. Even in his own way, with his reservations, there was a strong feeling in the heart of my Shadow Knight. I wanted things to have been resolved between them because I knew the pain of losing a loved one, but I also wanted to believe that a new era was beginning.

With the exception of the Pellegrinis, the strongest *famiglias* of the Cosa Nostra were in the hands of young men, with more modern ideas and perhaps willing to do something different.

It was probably an illusion, but I wished to believe that my child would be born into a less violent environment.

I placed my hand on my belly, thinking about the little one growing inside me. At the moment I did this, as if drawn to us like a magnet, Enrico almost smiled.

I had told him three days ago about the pregnancy, which I discovered after mornings of continuous nausea and a test done in the company of Deanna and Kiara, who were in town for Enrico's announcement as boss.

One already had a baby. Another was pregnant. They were the best companions I could have at that moment.

And the best part was seeing Enrico's eyes mist over and then feeling him cry as he hugged me, thanking me.

I was the one who needed to be grateful. He had saved me, given me a life, but in a much better way, and was still providing me with a family, friends, security.

What more did I need?

"Despite being a moment of pain, I have much to be grateful for." As if our minds were also connected, he began to speak of gratitude. "An insurmountable loss preceded a beautiful gift." Enrico pointed at me, extending his hand. I knew I would need to step forward at some point, so I was prepared for it.

He guided me to stand by his side, placing a protective arm around my shoulders.

"Not only do I have the best wife a man could have by my side, but there is a new family member on the way. A Preterotti heir."

This information led everyone to a round of even more enthusiastic applause.

With the rise of very young men to power, there was always a great fear that there wouldn't be heirs soon enough to keep the families in their places.

Dominic and Giovanni had no brothers, but both did not delay in "procreating." Enrico had Alessio in the line of succession, but he was not trustworthy, according to the organization's rules.

"In addition to my wife and my son, I also want to keep someone by my side whom I have complete trust in. Therefore, I appoint my brother, Alessio Preterotti, as my consigliere. He will be my right-hand man, my advisor."

This time, the applause wasn't as intense. Still, I imagined it would be a matter of time before Alessio proved his worth. Either that new version of the kind man I had met would win over the Cosa Nostra, or he seemed willing to go much further than before.

"To conclude, I would like to call to my side Dominic, Giovanni, and their wives." Knowing they would be called, both couples positioned themselves. Deanna, standing beside me, linked her arm with mine, smiling. We had become more than just sisters-in-law, which I greatly appreciated. "My friends, like brothers. They helped me when I needed it, helped my wife, and I am sure that together, we will make history within the Cosa Nostra. We will not disappoint anyone, we will be loyal, and we will no longer tolerate betrayals against our people. From today on, a new day will dawn for us. We will be untouchable."

Another round of applause, and I looked at the people, wondering that Enrico was giving that speech, but inside, both he and the others, Dominic and Giovanni, had one concern on their minds: Mattia was still at large. Promising revenge and wishing to destroy the Cosa Nostra as we knew it. He would not rest until he caused more harm and took power for himself. And I suspected he wanted much more than just the position of boss of a state. He wanted total control.

Depending on his speech, many would follow him. It was a matter of time before his plans would be revealed.

In the meantime, I would enjoy the moment.

I placed my hand on my belly again, until I felt Deanna lean in towards me to say:

"From traitor to queen of Los Angeles. Not bad..." she said with a smile, and I saw that Enrico, who was beside her, had heard.

He also placed his hand on my belly, smiling and whispering:
"Not bad at all, *Scarlatta*."

I sighed as he leaned in and gave me a kiss on the lips, even in front of everyone.

*That* pact was only between us—always trying to be the light for each other amidst the darkness. It was the agreement I would be most loyal to, from beginning to end.

Did you love *Scarred Loyalties*? Then you should read *Dangerous Vows*[1] by Lena Blake!

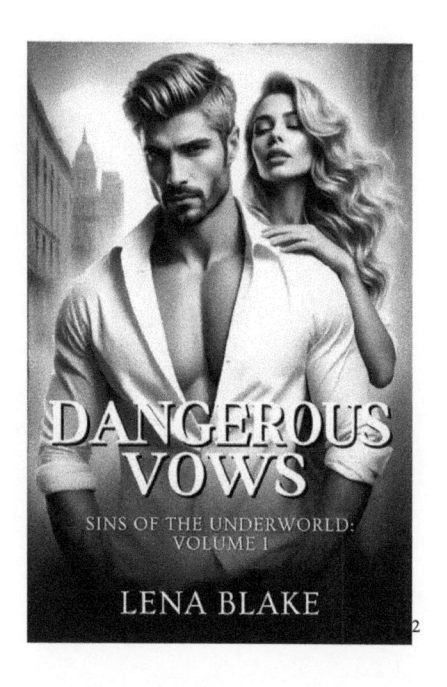

**Dangerous Vows** is a gripping mafia romance that blends passion, power, and betrayal.

Dominic, the ruthless head of the New York mafia, is a man who thrives on **control**. Cold, calculating, and dangerously **seductive**, he's willing to do whatever it takes to protect his **empire**. When his fiancée, a mafia princess, dies in a suspicious accident, Dominic is forced to marry her younger sister to maintain his grip on the **Cosa Nostra**.

Deanna was never meant to live in the mafia's shadow. Raised far from its deadly influence in Brazil, she's **fierce**, independent, and refuses to be controlled by anyone—especially not a man like Dominic.

---

1. https://books2read.com/u/3LBRAD

2. https://books2read.com/u/3LBRAD

But with her sick mother's life on the line, Deanna has no choice but to enter into a marriage of **convenience** with the man she **despises**.

As their worlds collide, **hatred** turns into a dangerous game of **temptation** and **desire**. Deanna fights to keep her heart guarded, while Dominic is determined to **break her down** and claim her for his own. But in the treacherous world of organized crime, where **loyalty** is a weapon and trust is a luxury, **love** may be the most dangerous gamble of all.

**Dangerous Vows** is a must-read for fans of **dark romance**, intense power dynamics, and **forbidden love**. If you're searching for a steamy mafia romance filled with tension, intrigue, and sizzling chemistry, this is the book for you. Will their **passion** destroy them or be the key to their **salvation**?

Perfect for readers who love mafia romance, **enemies-to-lovers**, and **strong-willed heroines**.

# Also by Lena Blake

**Chained by Fate**
Dark Collision
Beneath Her Armor

**Convenient Vows**
Surrender to the Sheikh
Sparks of Destiny
Taming the Storm

**Dangerous Contracts**
Surrendering to Shadows
Love's Dark Bargain
The Hidden Heir

**Irish Honor**
Dragon's Vow
Forbidden Flames
Forbidden Desires

Indecent Protection

**Laws of Passion**
Shattered by Secrets
Whirlwind of Desire
When Tornadoes Collide

**Mafia's Children**
Web of Seduction
Bound by Honor
Bound by Shadows
Fate's Gamble

**Sands of Passion**
In the Sheikh's Grasp
The Sheikh's Jewel
The Sheikh's Forbidden Bride
The Sheikh's Hidden Heart

**Sins of the Underworld**
Dangerous Vows
Scarred Loyalties

**Standalone**
Unintended Ties

The Ballerina's Keeper
Unplanned Obsession
Bound by Revenge
Forbidden Obsession
The Senator's Bargain
Dangerous Affections

## About the Author

**Lena Blake** is a storyteller whose novels immerse readers in a whirlwind of suspense, action, and adventure. With a keen eye for detail and a talent for crafting intricate plots, Lena captivates her audience with every twist and turn. Her compelling characters and atmospheric settings transport readers to thrilling worlds where danger lurks around every corner. When she's not writing, Lena enjoys exploring new destinations, drawing inspiration from her travels to weave into her gripping tales.

Milton Keynes UK
Ingram Content Group UK Ltd.
UKHW031902260924
448786UK00001B/83